A BOOK OF DEVILS AND DEMONS

Ruth Manning-Sanders was born in Swansea where she spent an exceptionally happy childhood reading omnivorously and acting with her sister in plays of their own composition. She was a Shakespearian scholar at Manchester University and while she was there married George Manning-Sanders, a Cornish artist. With him she covered the British Isles in a horse-drawn caravan and for two years shared the life of a travelling circus.

RUTH MANNING-SANDERS

A BOOK OF DEVILS
AND DEMONS

Cover illustration by Brian Froud
Text illustrations by Robin Jacques

A Piccolo Book

PAN BOOKS LTD
LONDON

First published in Great Britain 1970 by
Methuen & Co Ltd
This edition published 1973 by Pan Books Ltd,
33 Tothill Street, London SW1

ISBN 0 330 23717 9

By the same author in Piccolo
A BOOK OF WITCHES
A BOOK OF WIZARDS
A BOOK OF GIANTS
A BOOK OF DWARFS
A BOOK OF PRINCES AND PRINCESSES

Made and Printed in Great Britain by
Cox & Wyman Ltd, London, Reading and Fakenham

CONTENTS

FOREWORD

THERE ARE millions of little demons and millions of little devils; and there are a few big master demons who have kingdoms of their own, and rule over the little ones. But there is only one big master Devil, who is usually called Satan, and who rules over all the rest of the devils in his kingdom of Hell.

In some ways devils and demons are very much alike. Most of them are tricksters who delight in pestering human beings; and it is not easy to get the better of them since they have magic powers, can change themselves into any shape they fancy, can make themselves huge, can make themselves tiny, can make themselves invisible, can raise tempests, can fly through the air, can ride on whirlwinds, and even, if they so please, set half the world on fire. So that it is no wonder that the big Devil (Satan) has been described as 'the enemy of mankind'.

Well now, we may ask, what is the difference between a demon and a devil? Just this, it seems: you can't kill a devil, but you *can* kill a demon. The demon in the Hungarian story, *Ironhead*, may boast that he can wait to all eternity to get the hero, Peter, into his clutches: nevertheless in the end we find Ironhead being torn to pieces by Peter's three great dogs. And in the Transylvanian story, *The Demon's Daughter*, the invincible-seeming demon, after all his efforts to destroy the king's son, must end by himself ignominiously bursting into dust.

But no power on earth, or above the earth, or under the earth, can destroy Satan and his tribe of devils. They are, like the angels, immortal: they live forever. However, this is not as daunting as it sounds, for if you are brave and clever you can outwit even Satan himself – as you will find in the

Hungarian story, *Jack at Hell Gate*, and in the story of *The Blacksmith and the Devil*, which comes from Gascony.

And even this same Satan, enemy of mankind as he may be, has his kindlier moments. Long ago, a wandering tribe of shepherds, who tended their flocks in a wild country among the Carpathian mountains, had a story to tell of *The Little Red Mannikin* who befriends the poor man, Janko, when he is being imposed upon by his rich brother, Krok. And when he has eased Janko's lot for him, and left him happy and prosperous – who does this same Little Red Mannikin turn out to be? None other than Satan himself!

You will find another kindly disposed and merry little devil in the Danish story, *Tripple-Trapple*; and there is a pleasant forest demon in the Hungarian story, *The Peppercorn Oxen*. But as for the rest, both devils and demons, they are an unpleasant lot, and give our heroes and heroines any amount of trouble: whether in the Finnish story, *Something Wonderful*, or in the *Kittel-Kittel Car*, which comes from Alsace, or in *The Monkey Nursemaid*, which comes from India, or in the Norwegian story, *The Hill Demon*, or in the Danish story, *A Ride to Hell*.

However, none of these devils or demons are invincible. With courage, patience, and a fair share of that invaluable quality known as mother-wit, our heroes and heroines can in the end overcome all the wiles of both devils and demons, and pack them off about their tiresome business.

1 TRIPPLE-TRAPPLE

Once upon a time there was a merry little devil, and he changed himself into a big black pot with three legs, and set himself at the side of the road.

By and by a poor man comes walking along; the man had been out looking for work, but he hadn't found any. So he sees the pot and thinks, 'Well, that's something anyway!' And he picks it up and carries it home to his wife.

'Did you find any work?' says she.

'No,' says he. 'I called at a rich man's grand house and he set the dogs on me.'

'Oh, the wicked wretch!' cries she.

'But coming home I found a pot,' says he.

'Pooh, a pot,' says she, 'and nothing to put in it!'

'Maybe there'll be something to put in it by and by,' says the man. He sets the pot on the shelf. Then he goes out to look for work again, and the wife tidies up the kitchen.

So as she was clattering about with the broom, the pot up and spoke: 'Now I tripple-trapple off.'

'Where will you tripple-trapple to?' says she.

'To the house of the rich man who sets his dogs on the poor,' says the pot.

And it jumps off the shelf and away with it, *tripple-trapple, tripple-trapple*, on its three iron legs, till it comes to the rich man's grand house. And there it tripple-trapples into the kitchen.

'Ah ha!' thinks the cook. 'Here's a grand pot to make the porridge in!'

So she makes the porridge in the pot, and when the

porridge is well cooked, the pot says, 'Now I tripple-trapple off again.'

Says the cook, 'Where will you tripple-trapple to?'

'I tripple-trapple to the poor man with the porridge,' says the pot.

And it tripple-trappled off.

The poor man had come home again. No, he hadn't found any work, and his wife was crying. But when she saw the pot full of porridge, she wasn't crying any more, but laughing.

So the man and his wife had a good meal of porridge; and then the man cleaned the pot, put it back on the shelf, and went out.

All quiet in the kitchen for a while. And then the pot says, 'Now I tripple-trapple off.'

'Where will you tripple-trapple to this time?' says the wife.

'Back to the rich man's grand house,' says the pot. And it tripple-trapples away.

So it comes to the rich man's grand house, and into the dairy with it. And there was the dairymaid churning butter.

'Ah ha!' thinks she. 'Here's a fine big pot to put the butter in!'

And she filled the pot with butter.

And when it was full of butter to the brim, the pot said, 'Now I tripple-trapple off.'

'Where will you tripple-trapple to?' asks the dairymaid.

'To the poor man with the butter,' says the pot. And away with it, tripple-trapple, tripple-trapple, into the poor man's kitchen.

The poor man hadn't come home, but the wife was in the kitchen baking bread. When she saw the pot full of butter she danced for joy. 'Some we'll eat, and the rest we'll sell!' cried she. And she took the butter out of the pot, washed the pot, and put it on the shelf.

The pot stood quiet on the shelf for a little while. It was thinking. Then it said, 'Now I tripple-trapple off again.'

'Bless me!' says the wife. 'Where will you tripple-trapple to?'

'Back to the rich man's grand house,' says the pot. And it jumps off the shelf and away with it, *tripple-trapple, tripple-trapple*, on its three iron legs.

It comes to the rich man's grand house and tripple-trapples into the pantry; and there's the butler washing the silver.

'Oh ho!' thinks the butler. 'Here's a fine pot to wash the silver spoons in!' And he puts the silver spoons into the pot.

So, when all the spoons were in the pot, the pot said, 'Now I tripple-trapple off again.'

'Hey!' said the butler. 'You mustn't do that!' And he made a snatch at the pot.

But the pot tripple-trappled between the butler's feet. So the butler tumbled down and bruised his head. And by the time he'd picked himself up again, the pot had tripple-trappled off.

So the pot comes *tripple-trapple, tripple-trapple* into the poor man's kitchen. The poor man and his wife were spreading butter on their bread. When they saw the silver spoons they clapped their hands, took the spoons out of the pot, and put the pot back on the shelf.

The pot was tired. It had a little snooze. Then it woke up with a jerk and said, 'Now I tripple-trapple off again.'

'Where will you tripple-trapple to this time?' says the poor man.

'I tripple-trapple back to the rich man's grand house,' says the pot.

And away with it, *tripple-trapple, tripple-trapple,* to the rich man's grand house, and into a room where the rich man was counting out his money.

'Ha!' says the rich man. 'Here's a fine pot to put my gold in!' And he fills the pot brim-full with gold coins.

'Now I tripple-trapple,' says the pot. And off with it out of the rich man's house and along the road, *tripple-trapple, tripple-trapple*. The rich man runs after it. But can he catch

it? Not he! The faster he runs, the faster goes the pot on
its three iron legs, *tripple-trapple, tripple-trapple*. So they went,
went, went, the rich man running, the pot tripple-trappling, till
the rich man hadn't a breath left in him, and sank down on the
grass verge by the roadside. And when he'd caught his breath
again, the pot had vanished.

Then the pot comes, *tripple-trapple, tripple-trapple* into
the poor man's kitchen. The poor man had been out and sold

the silver spoons for a hamper of food. Now he was unpacking the hamper.

'Ah ha!' says he. 'Here's our pot come back!'

'What can it have brought this time?' says the wife.

But when they looked in the pot and saw that it was brim-full of gold pieces – oh my! didn't they hop and skip and jump for joy!

'Now we're rich, rich, rich!' cried they. And they took out the gold, hid it under a stone on the hearth, and put the pot back on the shelf.

The pot stood on the shelf for a long, long time. It was thinking. Then it jumped off the shelf and said, 'Now I tripple-trapple off again.'

'No need to do that, my pot,' says the man. 'We've got everything we want.'

'All the same, I tripple-trapple,' says the pot.

'And where will you tripple-trapple to?' says the wife.

'Back to the grand house of the rich man who sets his dogs on the poor,' says the pot. And off with it, *tripple-trapple, tripple-trapple.*

The rich man was sitting by his fish pond, catching carp. He had already caught a great many and they were lying on the bank. Along comes the pot, *tripple-trapple, tripple-trapple.*

'Ho!' thinks the rich man. 'That wretched pot again! But I'll get even with it this time!' So he calls out loud, 'Ha! Here's a fine pot to carry my fish home in!'

And he stoops over the pot, and makes as if to fill it with fish; but really he's filling it with mud.

Does he deceive the pot? Not he! And, my word, that pot's angry! It begins to swell and it begins to grow. It swells wider, wider, wider; it grows higher, higher, higher. And as the rich man is leaning over it, he's lifted high off his feet, and hangs there, clinging to the rim of the pot with both hands.

'Help! Help! Help!' cried the rich man, kicking and scrabbling. But the pot gives a jerk: down goes the rich man's head into the pot, down go his arms, down goes his body; now only his legs are sticking out. And kick those legs as they will, into the pot they must go, for the pot swells up round them. So there's the rich man, head down inside the pot, and buried in mud.

'Now I tripple-trapple,' says the pot.

And from inside the pot comes the rich man's voice, all mumbled up with mud. 'Where will you tripple-trapple to?'

'To HELL,' says the pot.

And it tripple-trapples off. And neither rich man nor pot was ever seen again.

2   THE DEMON'S DAUGHTER

There was a king who must go to war against his enemy. But the enemy's army was very great, and the king's army small. So, though the king's men fought bravely, they were driven back and back. Indeed it seemed as if the king must lose his army, his kingdom, and his all.

But just as the king was despairing, there came a whirlwind, and out of the whirlwind stepped a demon, holding an iron whip under his arm.

'What will you give me if I save your army for you?' says the demon.

'What do you ask?' says the king.

'Oh, a mere trifle,' says the demon. 'A new soul.'

Now the demon had but one foot, because his left leg ended in a hoof. And as on his one foot the demon was wearing a very old boot, the king thought that by a new soul, he meant a new sole for his boot, and he promised this willingly enough. 'As soon as ever I get home you shall have it,' said the king to the demon.

'Oh, I don't know that I want it now,' said the demon. 'In three times seven years will be time enough.'

'You shall have it whenever you wish,' said the king.

Then the demon went a little aside and cracked his iron whip four times: first to the west, then to the south, then to the east, then to the north. And with each crack of the whip, legions of armed demons came rushing. The demons fell upon the enemy army and routed it in half a minute. And the king rode home in triumph.

Now whilst the king had been away, the queen had given

birth to a baby boy. So what with his victory over the enemy, and the birth of his little son – well, in all the world you couldn't have found a happier king than that king.

Seven years passed; the baby prince grew into a merry child. Seven more years passed; the merry child grew into a handsome lad. Seven more years passed; the handsome lad grew into a young man, as good as he was handsome, as brave as he was good.

And on his twenty-first birthday the prince was hunting with his father in the forest, when there came a whirlwind, and out of the whirlwind stepped the demon.

'I have come for my new soul,' said the demon.

'You shall have it,' said the king. 'Come back with us to the palace, and the court shoemaker shall see to it at once.'

Then the demon let out such a screech of laughter that all the trees in the forest shuddered. 'It's not a sole for my boot I'm wanting,' said he. 'It's the soul of this young fellow here: the new soul that was born when my servants fought your battle for you.'

'No, *no*!' cried the king. 'I never promised you that!'

'Ah, but you did,' says the demon. 'And I still have my iron whip, and I can still call up my servants. Only this time it would be *your* kingdom they would destroy. So you'd best make up your mind to give me this young man, and be quick about it!'

The king fell on his knees, he sobbed, and besought the demon to have mercy. But the demon spurned the king with his cloven hoof, took his whip from under his arm, and said, 'I'll give you sixty seconds before I crack it.'

Then the prince raised his father from the ground and embraced him. 'Goodbye, dear Father,' said he. 'All will be well. The demon has no power to hurt me.'

'What, *what*, you young mirror of virtue!' screamed the demon. 'I'll teach you to regret that saying!' And he seized the prince and rushed with him through the air to his kingdom beyond the world.

And in that kingdom the demon showed the prince a flaming fiery furnace. 'Ah ha!' said the demon. 'The furnace is hot now, but by tomorrow morning it will be seven times hotter! And in that furnace you shall burn, young mirror of virtue, unless you can perform the task I shall set you.'

'I will endeavour to do whatever you ask of me,' said the prince.

Then the demon took the prince to his castle, led him into a small room and said, 'Look through the window. What do you see?'

'I see a mighty lake,' said the prince.

'Then this is your task,' said the demon. 'By tomorrow morning the lake must be dried up and changed into a hay field. And the hay must be mown and put into hay cocks ready for carting. If you can do this, I won't throw you into the fiery furnace. If you fail, you know what to expect.'

Then the demon went out, locked the door of the room, and took the key with him. And the prince sat at the window with his head in his hands. It seemed the demon had power to hurt him after all.

Now the demon had an adopted daughter, whom he had stolen out of the world when she was a baby, and of whom he was very proud. In fact, he spoiled her. And she went to the demon and said, 'Father, let me take the prince something to eat, for he must be very hungry.'

'What's the sense of his having food tonight, when he must die tomorrow?' said the demon.

'All the same, let me take it,' said she.

'H'm,' said the demon.

'*Please*, Father!'

'Well, don't you go and fall in love with him, you silly girl, or we shall have you weeping over his ashes.'

'I'm not going to fall in love with anyone!' said she. 'If it were only a hungry puppy, I should want to feed it.'

'Oh, all right, take your puppy some food, little soft head,' says the demon. And he gave her the key of the prince's room.

The girl put some food on a tray and carried it to the prince. And when she saw him, so handsome, so good, and so very, very miserable – oh dear me, she *did* fall in love with him on the spot.

'No, you shan't die tomorrow!' she cried. 'Come eat, drink, put away your grief. I will help you. Only show me a bright face in the morning!'

And she set down the tray and went out quickly, locking the door behind her.

And it was to the prince as if a ray of sunlight had come into the room and gone again, leaving him sadder than before.

The girl took the key back to the demon. 'Well,' says he, 'what did you make of your puppy?'

'I felt sorry for him,' said she.

'I said we should have you weeping over his ashes,' laughed the demon. 'But come now, sing me to sleep.'

So the girl sang the demon to sleep. And when he was snoring, she took two corks, and gently, gently put one in each of his ears. She picked up the iron whip from beside his bed, softly, softly tiptoed out of his room, and went to stand beside the lake. She cracked the iron whip four times: to the west, to the south, to the east, to the north. And with each crack the demon's kingdom trembled; there came a rushing and a hissing in the air, and from every side legions of demons came flying.

'What are your orders?' roared the demons.

'Dry up the lake,' said she, 'plant a hay meadow, mow the hay, and gather it into hay cocks. And before the first cock crows, let all be done.'

'We hear and we obey,' roared the demons.

'But quietly, quietly,' said the girl. 'We do not disturb those who sleep.'

And the demons, who had set about their work with a terrible clatter, now moved more quietly than a summer breeze.

The girl went back into the castle, tiptoed into the room where the demon lay sleeping, gently, gently drew the corks out of his ears, laid the whip by his bed, and tiptoed out again.

And all night long the prince sat at his window with his head in his hands. He was bidding farewell to life. Then came dawn. The first cock crew. The prince raised his head and stood up. 'If I am to die, I can at least die bravely!' said he. And he looked out of the window.

What did he see? No lake, but a wide meadow crowded with hay cocks!

Then the door flew open and in rushed the demon. 'You've beaten me this time!' he yelled. 'But tomorrow you shall have a taste of my red hot coals!' And he seized the prince and carried him through the air to the top of a high mountain. On the top of the mountain was a forest. 'Tonight,' said the demon, 'you must cut down this forest, and cord the trees into bundles ready to cart away. And where the forest has been, you must plant a vineyard, with the grapes ripe and ready to gather.'

'What you demand of me is not possible!' said the prince.

'Very well,' said the demon, 'you shall taste of my red hot coals.'

And he carried the prince back to the castle, pushed him into a room with a window that looked on the mountain, and locked the door on him.

Then came the demon's daughter with food for the prince.

'Oh,' said she, 'I looked to see a bright face this morning, but I find you still sad!'

'How should I not be sad?' said the prince. And he told her the demon's orders.

'Have I not helped you once?' said she. 'And shall I not help you again? Repay me with a smile – it's all I ask.'

So the prince smiled, and took her hand and kissed it.

And the girl smiled and went away, locking the door behind her.

That night the girl again sang the demon to sleep, corked up his ears, took his whip, and went to stand outside the castle gates. She cracked the whip four times, and the legions of demons came rushing. She told them what they must do, and most vehemently did they set about it. Before the first cock crew the forest was cut down, and the felled tree trunks bound into bundles. And where the forest had been was a vineyard with grapes ripe and ready for gathering.

And when the demon looked out and saw what was done, he was like to bust with rage.

He rushed to the prince. 'Who taught you wizardry?' he roared. 'You have beaten me twice, but you shan't beat me a third time! Tonight, out of sand and nothing else, you must build me a church. On the church must be a dome, and on the dome a cross.' And he whirled out of the room, locking the door behind him.

Then came the girl, bringing food.

The prince was smiling. 'If the girl could work two magics, she can surely work a third!' he thought. But when he told her of this third task, the girl looked very grave.

'This is indeed a heavy order!' said she. 'I doubt if it can be done. But I will try.' And she went away, locking the door behind her.

So on that third night the girl again sang the demon to sleep, corked up his ears, took the iron whip from beside his bed, and went out. She cracked the whip to the west, to the south, to the east, to the north: the earth trembled, the sky echoed, and through the air legions of demons came rushing.

'What are your orders?' they roared.

'Build me a church out of pure sand,' says she. 'On the church must be a dome, and on the dome a cross.'

But the demons shivered and shrank. 'We cannot! We cannot build a church!' they wailed. 'We cannot build a church out of stone or iron, much less out of sand!'

'You shall do as I tell you,' cried the girl. And she cracked the whip again and again. So the demons set to work, gathering up the sand, and the girl stood over them, cracking the whip. And at every crack of the whip, the sweat poured off the demons so that the sand formed into clods. And with these clods they began to build.

The church was a quarter-built. And then it fell down, and the demons had to begin again. And now the church was half-built, and again it fell down, and the demons had to begin once more. The girl cracked the whip and cracked the whip till pains shot through her right arm. She took the whip in her left hand, and cracked on and on. Now the demons had the church three-quarters built; but again it fell down. The girl changed the whip from her left hand to her right, and cracked on and on. The demons began to build yet a fourth time. They sweated, they groaned. Now they had the church all but finished; the dome was up, the church lacked only the cross. But when the demons tried to set up the cross, the whole church collapsed.

The girl glanced up at the sky. The stars were paling, and in the east there glimmered the merest streak of light. The girl put the whip under her arm and bade the demons begone. They whimpered, rose into the air, and vanished. The girl ran back into the castle, and unlocked the door of the prince's room.

The prince was sleeping peacefully. He had faith in the girl this time! But she shook him into wakefulness. 'Up, up!' she cried. 'The church cannot be built, but I will still save you! I will change myself into a white horse, you shall mount on my back, and I will carry you home.' She thrust the whip into his hand, and ran out. The prince hurried after her. But in his hurry he dropped the whip.

The dawn brightened, a cock woke, flapped his wings and crowed, *Cock-a-doodle-doo!*

Cock-a-doodle-doo! From near and far the cocks were crowing. But the demon did not hear them. He snored and snored. Then a beam of sunlight fell across his face and he woke. Daylight! He looked from the window. There lay the meadow crowded with hay cocks; there stood the mountain shorn of its forest and planted with a vineyard. But the church – there was no church, only tumbled heaps of sand.

The demon let out such a scream of triumph that the whole castle trembled. But something was wrong with that scream – he could scarely hear it. And what was this, what was this? His household should be at work, but all seemed silent. Had he gone deaf in the night? He put his hands to his ears, and drew out two great corks. And then he let out a screech that did indeed almost deafen him. He looked round for his whip. The whip had gone! He rushed to the prince's room; the door stood open, the prince was not there. But the whip was lying on the floor.

Snatching up the whip, the demon ran out and stood before the castle gates. He cracked the whip four times: to the east, to the south, to the west, to the north. But the earth did not tremble, nor the sky echo; only there came a whimpering in the air, and down dropped a legion of weary demons. 'What *again*, Master?' whimpered the demons. 'We have worked all night, and we are very tired. Are we to have no rest?'

'Worked all night!' shouted the demon. 'Who commanded you to work all night?'

'Your daughter, Master, at your orders.'

'I am betrayed!' screamed the demon. And he gave a leap and rose high into the air to look over all his kingdom. Far away he saw a white horse galloping across a plain. And on the white horse's back he saw the prince.

'After them!' he called to his servant demons as he shot down to earth again. 'Arm and after a white horse and its rider. Bring them back dead or alive!'

Hey presto! The sky became black with flying demons, and the sound of their rushing came to the ears of the galloping horse.

'Look back,' said the horse to the prince. 'What do you see?'

'I see a great cloud coming this way.'

'That is my father's army,' said the white horse. 'We are lost unless you do exactly as I tell you. I will change myself into a church, and you into a priest. You must stand before the altar and sing without ceasing. When you are spoken to, you must not answer.'

Immediately the white horse and the prince vanished. There on the plain stood a great church; and at the altar in the church stood a priest, who sang and sang, '*Lord be with us! Lord protect us!*'

The crowd of flying demons came down to stand before the church. They peered through the open door, but they dared not venture in. The voice of the priest at the altar rose clear and tuneful, '*Lord be with us! Lord protect us!*' The demons stood enthralled. They listened for a long time; then they called, 'Sir priest, have you seen a rider on a white horse pass this way?'

'*Lord be with us! Lord protect us!*' sang the priest.

'Sir priest, sir priest, have you seen a rider on a white horse?'

'*Lord be with us! Lord protect us!*' The priest never paused one moment in his singing. So the demons rose up into the air and flew on. They flew to the very edge of their master's kingdom. They saw neither horse nor rider. So they turned and flew back to the demon's castle. And by the time they got back it was night.

'Well, did you find them?' yelled the demon.

'No, Master, we did not.'

Then the demon flew into such a rage that his eyes, and his mouth, his ears, and his nostrils shot out flames. His servants fled from before his face; and the demon spent the night running upstairs and down, and in and out of the castle, for his anger wouldn't let him rest.

First thing in the morning he leaped straight up into the air, high, high, higher, till he could see over all his kingdom. Far away, seven hundred miles away, he saw the church, and from far away there came to his ears the faint sound of a singing voice that cut him to the soul.

Down he dropped to earth again and cracked his whip. He cracked it till the air was dark with his demon servants. 'Off!

Off!' he yelled. 'Seize upon that church and pull it to the ground! Bring me one stone of the church, and bring me, dead or alive, that rascally priest who sings before the altar!'

Off through the air rushed the crowd of demons. But the church had gone, and the priest had gone; and along a green valley galloped the prince on the white horse. 'I hear a whistling in the air,' said the white horse. 'Look behind you. What do you see?'

'I see a bigger and a blacker cloud speeding this way.'

'That is my father's army,' said the white horse. 'We are lost unless you do exactly as I say. I will change myself into a tree, and you into a little golden bird, perched on my topmost branch. Sing, sing, little golden bird, and never stop singing. Let nothing turn you from your song!'

Then the white horse vanished, and the prince vanished. In the green valley stood a tree, and on the topmost branch of the tree perched a little golden bird that sang and sang, *'Frighten me not! Frighten me not! Frighten me not!'*

The flying cloud of demons swept on. They had come seven hundred miles now from the plain where the church had stood. They hovered above the green valley, and came down to stand under the tree. They gazed up at the little golden bird, that sang and sang, *'Frighten me not! Frighten me not! Frighten me not!'*

'When it stops singing we will ask it for news,' said the demons. But the little golden bird didn't stop singing. So the demons called up to it, 'Little golden bird, has a rider on a white horse passed this way?'

'Frighten me not! Frighten me not! Frighten me not!' sang the little golden bird.

And since it wouldn't stop singing, the demons rose up into the air again, and sped on. They flew to the very end of their master's kingdom, and finding neither horse nor rider, they turned and flew back. And by the time they reached their master's castle it was night.

'Well, have you brought them?' yelled the demon.

'No, master, we have not. We could not find them.'

So the demon spent that night also in raging to and fro. And in the morning he leaped straight up into the air, high, higher, till he could see over all his kingdom. Far away he saw the tree in the green valley, and from far away, and very softly, there came to his ears the song of the little golden bird that cut him to the soul.

'Ah! I'll get you yet!' he screamed. And he shot down to earth and cracked his whip – cracked it again and again, till the air about him was dark with hovering demons. 'Hurry! Hurry!' he yelled. 'Go to the green valley, cut down the tree, bring me back one twig of the tree, and bring the little golden bird, dead or alive.'

The dark cloud of demons flew off. They came to the green valley, but the tree had gone, and the golden bird had gone.

The rider on the white horse had travelled seven hundred miles from the green valley when the white horse said, 'I hear a roaring in the air behind us. Look back. What do you see?'

'I see a bigger and blacker and more terrible cloud speeding this way.'

'Those are the flying hosts of my father,' said the white horse. 'I will change myself into a cornfield, and you into a quail to run to and fro among the corn. Run, run, continually, and sing without stopping, or we are lost.'

Then the white horse vanished, and the prince vanished. And the sun glittered down on a field of golden corn, in which a little quail ran to and fro, and sang, sang, sang.

And swift through the air rushed the flying hordes of demons. Seven hundred miles they had flown to the plain where the church had stood; another seven hundred miles they had flown to the green valley; and yet another seven hundred miles beyond the green valley they flew, but they saw neither white horse nor rider. They saw only a wide field of glittering corn.

The demons came down to stare in astonishment at the glittering corn. And they saw the little quail running through the corn, to and fro, and never stopping. And all the time that little quail was singing out, '*Wit with us! Wit with us! Wit with us!*'

'When the little bird stands still and ceases to call, we will question it,' said the demons.

But the little bird didn't stand still. To and fro it ran through the corn on its short legs, and all the time it was singing out, '*Wit with us! Wit with us! Wit with us!*'

'Have you seen a rider on a white horse pass this way?' called the demons at last.

'*Wit with us! Wit with us! Wit with us!*' sang the quail, running through the corn on its short legs.

So the demons rose into the air again and flew on for another seven hundred miles, and came to the boundaries of the demon's kingdom; and so, seeing neither horse nor rider, went back the way they had come. And when they reached the demon's castle, it was night.

'Have you brought me a twig of that tree, have you brought me the golden bird?' roared the demon.

'No, Master, we have not. We saw neither tree nor bird.'

'Fools! Idiots! Good-for-nothings!' shouted the demon. 'Tomorrow I must go myself!'

All that night the demon kept springing up into the air and down again, trying to pierce through the darkness with the sparks from his eyes. But the sparks only glittered in the darkness round him, making the night beyond their reach more black. When the morning came he was leaping higher than ever: saw, three times seven hundred miles away, a faint golden streak that was the field of corn; and heard, soft as a whisper, the song of the quail that cut him to the heart.

'I will have you this time!' he screamed, and set off through the air faster than any wind that blows.

But the field of corn had gone, and the quail had gone; and the prince on the white horse was galloping, galloping. Only seven more miles of the demon's kingdom now lay before them. Only seven more miles and they would be safe!

But behind them now they heard the roaring as of a mighty storm, and the white horse said, 'Look back – what do you see?'

'I see a black spot in the sky, a spot blacker than night, and out of it come darts of fiery lightning.'

'Alas! Alas! It is my father. I will change myself into a pond of pure milk, and you into a duck. Swim round in the middle of the pond, keep your eyes down, and never turn your head or look towards the bank, however much you may be coaxed and flattered.'

Then the white horse vanished, and the prince vanished. And in the middle of a pond of pure milk, a duck swam round and round. The demon flew down to stand beside the pond. He was not deceived. He knew well enough what the pond was, and what the duck was. But he dared not venture into the pond, because demons drown in pure milk. So he stood on the bank and began to speak honeyed words.

'Dear, pretty little duck, why do you swim round and round in that nasty puddle of milk? Come, little duck, come to the bank. I have a cake for you, my pretty one!'

But the duck kept its head turned away, and went on swimming round and round in the middle of the pond.

'Oh ho! Shy, pretty little duck! At least lift up your head that I may see your beautiful eyes!'

But the duck kept its eyes down and its head turned away. So the demon ran round the pond and round the pond, coaxing and speaking honeyed words. And still the duck swam round and round in the middle of the pond, and kept its eyes down and its head turned away. So at last the demon gave three loud yells and transformed himself into a gigantic goose. And in three gulps the gigantic goose swallowed down the pond of milk, duck and all.

And then, feeling mightily full and heavy, that goose began to waddle away home.

But the goose hadn't taken many steps before the milk inside him began to boil. And the goose began to swell. He swelled and swelled and swelled: he was frightened. He felt so hot and heavy that he could scarcely stagger. 'Oh me, if I were only home!' he sighed. And still the milk boiled and frothed and foamed inside him. And he hadn't waddled more than a few more stumbling steps when suddenly there was a loud crack.

Crack! It was all up with that goose. He burst into a million pieces: the pieces turned to dust. And there by the dust stood the prince and girl, hand in hand.

So hand in hand they walked out of the demon's kingdom. And hand in hand they walked on through the blessed world, till they came to the palace of the king, the prince's father. And if there had been great sadness in that palace, there was now as great rejoicing.

The prince and the girl were married next day. And never anywhere on earth was there a merrier wedding.

3 SOMETHING WONDERFUL

A king had an only son, who wasn't exactly lazy, and who wasn't exactly stupid; but he was the kind of lad who seemed to take no interest in anything except his own thoughts.

And the king said to the prince, 'My lad, this won't do! Please remember that you will become king some day. And how can you govern a kingdom if you sit there dreaming, and hardly know the difference between a throne and a footstool?'

'Well,' said the prince, 'there isn't such a wonderful difference, is there? You can sit on both of them.'

Then the king got angry and cried out, 'Wonderful! Wonderful! Is there anything in the world that you consider wonderful?'

'I don't know,' said the prince. 'There might be.'

'Then be off with you and find it!' snapped the king. 'And don't you dare come back without this *something wonderful*!'

So the prince set out. He walked, walked, and came into a wood, where there were many tall straight trees, and a few whose branches were crooked and twisted.

'Now I wonder,' thought the prince, 'why it is that some of these trees grow straight and some of them crooked . . . Ha! I *wonder! I wonder!* Then surely here is something wonderful!' And he broke off one of the twisted branches and one of the straight ones, took them back to the palace, and threw them on the floor in the king's parlour.

Then he sits and looks out of the window; and by and by in comes the king.

'What, back again? Have you then found something wonderful?'

'Yes, father. There on the floor.'

The king was angry. 'You fool! *This* is not wonderful!'

'Oh, isn't it? It made *me* wonder.'

'Dolt! Imbecile!' cried the king. 'Be off with you again! And if you come back without bringing me something wonderful, I'll – I'll – I'll . . .'

The king didn't say what he'd do. He choked with rage and stamped out.

And the prince set off once more.

He walked, walked, walked, and he came onto a lonely moor. He hadn't thought to bring any food with him, and by this time he was very hungry. And what should he see on the top of a great stone but a jug of milk and a loaf of bread and a plate of meat.

'Well now,' said the prince, 'this *is* wonderful! But I don't think I'm going to take these things back to my father. I think I'm going to eat them all up!' And he stretched out his hand to take the milk and the food off the stone.

But the milk and the food vanished.

'And that is more than wonderful!' said the prince. 'First something – then nothing! But I can't go back to my father with a handful of nothing!'

And he walked on. But oh me – he was hungry! And he hadn't taken more than a step or two when he turned to look longingly at the stone. Well – would you believe it? There again on the top of the stone stood the bottle of milk, the loaf of bread, and the plate of meat.

The prince ran back to the stone. He stretched out his hand to take up the loaf of bread. But it disappeared under his hand, and so did the milk, and so did the meat. And from under his feet, where the shadow of the stone lay, there came a chuckling laugh.

'I'll teach you to play tricks on me!' cried the prince. And he drew his sword and stabbed at the shadow of the stone.

The shadow gave a screech; and there by the stone lay a little

blue demon, with one of his big bat's ears pinned to the ground
by the point of the prince's sword.

'Oh! Oh! Oh!' screamed the demon. 'It hurts! It hurts! Set
me free! Set me free!'

'Not unless you give me some food,' said the prince.

Then the demon, wriggling and sobbing, took a satchel from
his shoulder and held it out to the prince. 'Here you are,' he
sobbed. 'You have only to say:

> *Give me food, little satchel,*
> *Give me drink, little satchel,*

and the food and the drink will appear.'

'So you tell me,' said the prince. 'But how do I know you're
not lying?'

'Prove it! Prove it!' sobbed the little demon. 'Take it in your
hands and prove it!'

So the prince took the satchel and said:

> *'Give me food, little satchel,*
> *Give me drink, little satchel.'*

And immediately out of the satchel came all sorts of delicious
things to eat and drink.

The prince ate and ate; but he still kept the demon pinned to
the ground, lest the food should disappear again. And that little
demon wept and moaned all the time the prince was eating.

'You can keep the satchel if only you'll set me free,' sobbed
the little demon.

'But what shall I do with the dishes and goblets?' said the
prince.

'Oh, just say:

> *Little satchel, little satchel,*
> *Pack up the plates and goblets once again,*

moaned the little demon.

So the prince, when he had eaten and drunk till he was full, said that, and the empty goblets and the dishes went back into the satchel. Then the prince drew his sword out of the little blue demon's ear; and where the little demon had been lying, there was nothing but the shadow of the stone.

The prince now decided to take the satchel back to his father. 'For surely,' he thought, 'this *is* something wonderful!' And he turned to go home. But he couldn't find the way home, and he wandered on all day, quite lost, till in the evening he came to the bank of a great river.

There was a little hut by the river, and the prince thought, 'It will soon be black night. I will go into the hut and sleep till morning.'

The door of the hut was wide open. But when the prince thought to go into the hut, that door slammed in his face. And shake it and kick it as he might, he couldn't open it.

So he ordered his satchel to give him some supper; and when he had eaten and drunk, he curled himself up outside the hut to sleep. But the night was cold, he couldn't sleep. He lay shivering and listening to the gurgle of the river. It seemed to him that the river was laughing at him. And then it seemed that the laughter wasn't coming from the river, but from somewhere behind him. And surely he had heard that chuckling laugh before!

He leaped to his feet and looked round. The hut stood up dark and clear in the moonlight, *and the hut door was wide open*. The prince ran to go inside the hut, but no sooner had he reached the door than it slammed in his face. And from it came that chuckling laugh.

'So you're at your tricks again, are you?' cried the prince, drawing his sword and giving the door a stab.

The door gave a screech. And there, pinned to the door by one shoulder, was the little blue demon.

'Oh! Oh!' screamed the little blue demon. 'It hurts! It hurts! Set me free!'

'You just make that door open!' said the prince.

So then the door swung wide, with the little demon still pinned to it by the prince's sword.

'Now set me free,' sobbed the little demon.

'But why should I set you free?' said the prince. 'You'll only play tricks on me again. Why do you do it?'

'I can't help it,' sobbed the little demon. 'It's my nature. But if you'll set me free I'll give you a better sword than the one you have: a magic sword that will cut off the head of anyone you tell it to: a sword that will cut off all the heads in the world at your command.'

'I'd like to see that sword,' said the prince.

The little demon snapped his fingers: there came a clang in the air, and a sword fell onto the ground at the prince's feet. It looked an ordinary sword enough, with a blade somewhat rusty. The prince picked it up. 'How do I know it will do as you say?' he asked.

'Prove it, prove it!' cried the demon. 'Tell it to cut off my head!'

'I don't know that I want to do that,' said the prince, 'even if you are a little nuisance! No, I think I'd better leave you pinned to the door.'

The little demon took a whistle from his pocket. 'I'll give you this whistle,' said he. 'You've only to blow on it to get anything you want. If you cut off my head and kill me, you've only to blow the whistle and say, "Make him alive again." And the whistle will do it.'

'That indeed would be something wonderful!' said the prince.

Then the prince released the little demon from the door, and said to the rusty sword, 'Cut off his head.' The sword gave a leap, and off rolled the demon's head. Then the prince blew the whistle. 'Now make the little rascal come alive,' said he.

The little demon's head leaped onto his body again, and that little demon jumped up alive and well.

'But mind you,' said the prince, 'if you come playing tricks

on me ever again, I'll have your head off, *and I won't put it on again!* So now, be off with you!... But stay, tell me first how I can get home.'

'Keep turning to the left and you'll get there,' said the little demon. 'And may we never meet again!' he cried with a scream of rage. Then he disappeared through the floor of the hut.

By now the sun had risen; it was a clear morning. The prince came out of the hut, and turned to the left. He walked along, and he walked along, and wherever there was a turning to the left, he took it. By and by he came to a big stony field; and beyond the field he could see the king's palace glittering in the sun.

'Well, surely now I have something wonderful to take to my father!' thought he. 'And not only one thing, but three things. So now to give him a surprise!' And he blew his whistle and said, 'Build me a castle on this stony field.'

Hey presto! There stood the castle.

The prince blew the whistle again. 'Let this stony field be a great green meadow, and let flocks and herds be grazing on it!' said he.

Hey presto! There was the great green meadow, where flocks of sheep and herds of cattle grazed.

The prince blew the whistle yet again. 'Let there be a bridge arching over the meadow from this castle to the king's palace,' said he.

Hey presto! There was the bridge.

And the king came out of his palace and stood on the steps, and saw the castle, and the meadow, and the great bridge. 'What can be the meaning of this?' said he. 'What wizardry has built this castle, and raised this bridge, and turned the stony field into a meadow where flocks and herds are grazing?' And he called messengers to him, and bade them ride across the bridge.

'Whatever people you meet with,' said he, 'summon them to appear before me.'

So the messengers rode over the bridge. And when the prince saw them coming, he blew his whistle and said, 'Let the grass blades of this meadow become people, and let the people go to stand before the bridge.'

Then up from the meadow sprang a multitude of men dressed in green. The men had green faces and green hands – they were green all over. And they went to stand at the entrance to the bridge. And when the king's messengers saw the green men, they were frightened, and fled back to the king.

'Well,' said the king, 'did you meet with any people?'

'Oh, sire,' cried the messengers, 'we did; but we cannot tell what manner of people they may be.'

Said the king, 'Did you summon them to appear before me?'

'Oh, sire, we dared not. We were frightened and fled.'

'Is that the way you carry out my orders?' cried the king. 'Begone, you cowards!' And he called up his whole army, and bade the army march across the bridge to summon the green men to appear before him.

So the army marched off across the bridge. But when they got to the other side, the green men had gone, and there was only one man standing by the bridge, and that was the prince.

Said the prince, 'Go back, and bid the king come here. Say I have something wonderful to show him.'

The army marched back and told the king. And then they marched again across the bridge, with the king riding at their head.

So, when they were all gathered in the meadow, the prince laid his satchel on the ground and said:

> *'Give us food, little satchel,*
> *Give us drink, little satchel.'*

And immediately out of the satchel came all sorts of delicious things to eat and drink, in such quantity that the whole army was fed.

And when they had all eaten, the prince said:

> *'Little satchel, little satchel,*
> *Pack up the plates and goblets once again.'*

And immediately all the empty goblets and dishes went back into the satchel.

'Is this a wonder?' said the prince to the king.

And the king answered, 'Yes, it is a wonder.'

'Ah, but I will show you something still more wonderful,' said the prince. And he waved his rusty sword and ordered it to cut off every head except the king's head and his own.

The sword clanged. There lay the army: heads in one place, bodies in another.

'Is this a wonder?' said the prince.

The king wrung his hands and wailed. 'Why did you kill all my soldiers? I thank you for your wretched wonders! If you summon me to see any more wonders like this – I'm off home!'

'Wait, wait!' said the prince. And he took the whistle out of his pocket. 'Heads on shoulders again,' said he. And he blew the whistle.

Then every soldier's head leaped onto its body again, and the whole army stood up, alive and well.

'Is that something wonderful?' said the prince.

'Yes, it is something wonderful,' said the king. 'But I have seen enough. Show me no more of your wonders, or I shall die of fright! I admit that when your time comes to reign you will make a powerful king, even though you don't see much difference between a throne and a footstool.'

'It's all according to how you look at things,' said the prince.

And he went back with the king, his father, to the palace. Nor did the king ever find fault with him again. Indeed, the king was now rather afraid of his son; though of course he did his best not to show it.

There was a gypsy called Graf, and he went into the forest with two poor men to cut wood. *Chop, chop, chop,* and *chop, chop, chop* – they get tired and hot and hungry. Says one of them, 'If there should be a spirit in this wood, and should that spirit grant us each a wish, what would we ask for?'

'I,' said the other poor man, 'would wish that when I got home I should find on my table a dish of fried sausages and a big white loaf of bread.'

'And I,' said the first poor man, 'would wish that when I got home I should find on my table a dish of curd cakes. And now, Graf, let's hear your wish!'

Graf laughs. He doesn't believe in spirits in woods, not he! Nor yet in wishes coming true. So he makes a joke of it and says, 'Oh, I would wish that when I got home I should have twelve little sons all born on the same day.'

Well, the three of them set to work again, *chop, chop, chop.* And when it drew towards evening, they each one made a bundle of such wood as they could carry, and leaving the rest to be fetched away in the morning, they set off for their homes.

What did one poor man see when he went into his house? He saw a dish of curd cakes on the table.

What did the other poor man see when he went into his house? A dish of fried sausages and a big white loaf on his table.

What did Graf see when he went into his house? He saw the village midwife bustling about the kitchen.

So he says good evening to her, and goes to put his bundle of wood down in a corner.

'Don't put it there!' shrieks the midwife. 'Can't you see the baby?'

Well, it was a bit dark by this time; but Graf did seem to see something in the corner, so he goes to lay his bundle down in another corner.

'Don't put it there!' shrieks the midwife. 'There's another baby!'

Dear me, so there was! Graf went to lay his bundle down on the hearth.

'Don't put it there!' shrieks the midwife. 'Don't you see the babies?'

And Graf did see the babies, two of them, lying on the hearth, with the firelight flickering on their little bald heads.

'Well then, I'll put the bundle down here,' says Graf, moving a bit away from the hearth.

But 'Don't put it there!' shrieks the midwife. And sure enough Graf sees another baby, lying just where he was going to put down his bundle. And it's 'Well, then I'll put it here, or here, or here,' from Graf, and one shriek after another from the midwife, 'Don't put it there, or there, or there, you clumsy fellow! Can't you see the babies?'

'Well, then,' says Graf, 'where can I put it?'

'You can't put it anywhere,' says the midwife. 'There's no room.'

'Thunder and lightning!' says Graf. 'How many babies are there?'

'Twelve,' says the midwife, 'and all boys.'

Graf gets frightened. 'Thunder and lightning!' says he. 'Then I'm the thirteenth man here! Nay, I can't be the thirteenth man, for that's unlucky! I won't stay here! I'd rather be a fire-stoker in hell!'

And he ran out.

But scarcely had he got outside the door, than a limping devil sprang out of the ground, seized him by the collar, and carried him off to hell as a fire-stoker.

Well, the twelve gypsy babies grew up, and fine lads they were, the pride and joy of their mother. So one day, the latest born, whose name was Jack, said, 'Mother, where's our father gone to all this time?'

So his mother tells him his father's gone to hell, and she begins to cry a bit.

Says Jack, 'Well, Mother, if that's the case, no need to cry about it. I'll soon find him and bring him home.'

So Jack sets out. He walks and walks; he walks all round the world, asking folk to tell him the way to hell. But nobody can tell him, for it seems that nobody knows; or, if they do know, they won't say. So he comes to a place where there's a big tree growing, and the tree's so old that there's a hollow in it near the ground. And since it's coming on night time, Jack creeps into the hollow, thinking to curl up and go to sleep there.

But he doesn't get time to curl up, because the hollow goes down and down, right through the earth, and Jack finds himself slipping. And when he's done slipping, he comes out on to a bare plain, and at the far end of the plain he sees hell gate.

So he goes across the plain, and he hasn't gone far when he meets a regiment of soldiers.

'Where are you going, gypsy lad?' says the captain of the regiment.

'I'm seeking my father, and I'm going to hell.'

'Oh, but you can't go there!' says the captain. 'We've just been, and we couldn't get in. The devils have stolen our king's daughter, and the king has promised half the kingdom to the one who can get her back. So naturally we've been having a try; but the devils won't even open the gate. So there's nothing for us to do but march home again. And you'd better do the same.'

'March home, is it?' says Jack. 'March home, when I've come as far as this? Certainly I won't march home!' And he went on his way and came to hell gate.

'Is Satan at home?' shouts he, knocking on the gate.

'No, he isn't,' shrilled a crowd of little devils from inside.

'Well, then,' says Jack, 'you give me out my father!'

'We shan't, we shan't, we shan't!' shouted the devils.

'Well, then, if you won't give me Father, hand me out a spade,' says Jack.

'What do you want with a spade?'

'Oh, just to dig a bit.'

The devils laughed. They thought Jack was crazy. But they handed him out a spade, to see what he'd do with it.

So Jack took the spade, and began to pace backwards and forwards: so many paces to the right, so many paces back, so many paces to the left, so many paces forward, and marking off his paces with the spade, till he'd got a great rectangle drawn there on the ground outside hell gate.

The devils watched him through the bars of the gate. They were mocking him and squealing with laughter. 'What d'you think you're doing there, you crazy gypsy boy?'

'Well,' says Jack, 'I'm just marking out a plan. I'm going to build a church here against the gate, so that none of you that are in hell can get out, and none of you who happen to be out of hell can get in again.'

'Oh! Oh! Oh! You can't do that!'

'Ho, can't I?' says Jack. 'I can and I will, unless you hand over my father.'

Then the devils were so frightened that they ran and fetched Graf and pushed him through the gate. 'Here's your old man!' they cried. 'Now go away!' And they slammed the gate again.

'How d'you do, Father?' says Jack. 'I'm proud to make your acquaintance! But, ho, ho!' he laughs, 'we're not going away yet! We're not going to move one step from here,' says he to the devils, 'till you bring out the king's daughter.'

'We daren't, we daren't!' wailed the devils. 'Don't ask it, gypsy boy! If we let the princess go, Satan will bury us in ice and freeze our limbs off! We'll give you gold, we'll give you silver – heaps of it, as much as you and your old father can carry – if only you'll go away!'

But Jack says, 'I don't want your gold, and I don't want your silver, I want the king's daughter. So come on now, hand her over!'

'Oh! Oh! Wait at any rate till Satan comes home!'

'I shan't wait another minute. Will you bring her, or will you not bring her? If you don't,' says Jack, taking up the spade, 'I shall build here against the gate such a church that Satan himself will not be able to get into hell again. No, never, never! Now we'll get out the foundations,' says he. And he begins to dig.

The devils screamed and ran. They fetched the princess and pushed her through the gate. 'Now will you go?' they cried, slamming the gate again.

'Yes, we'll be off now,' says Jack. 'Good morning all!' And he gave his right hand to the princess, and his left hand to his father; and so, hand in hand, they walked away across the plain.

They hadn't gone very far when Satan came flying over their heads on his way back to hell. Satan had wrapped a black cloud round himself; so he didn't see Jack, nor Jack's father, nor the princess. He whizzed in through hell gate like an arrow from a bow, and as soon as he got inside he called out, 'Where's the princess? Bring me the princess that I may marry her!'

So then the devils wailed like a whole menagerie full of cats and parrots. 'We've given her to the gypsy lad – boo hoo! – because he said if we didn't he'd build a church at hell gate, so that – boo hoo! boo hoo! – none of us could go out or come in!'

'Fools!' bellowed Satan. 'How could he build a church? He had nothing to build it with!' and he shouted for his Swift Runner. 'Off after them, my Swift Runner! Fetch the princess back!'

So Swift Runner set off and overtook Jack and the others in a twinkling. 'Give me back the princess!' he shouts.

'Ho! Ho!' says Jack. 'Give her back, is it? I'm not going to give anything back unless you can prove you're a better man than I am. It'll be time enough to talk after that.'

'Well, then,' says Swift Runner, 'I'll race you across the plain.'

'Nay,' says Jack. 'I don't run races with such a poor little shrimp as you! It wouldn't be fair. But tell you what,' says he, casting his eyes round and seeing a hare under a bush, 'you can race with my young brother. If you can beat him, you shall have the princess back.'

'And where is your young brother?'

'Oh, just having a snooze under the bush yonder. Give him a shout and he'll wake up.'

So Swift Runner went to the bush and shouted. The hare started up and off. The hare ran, ran, ran. Swift Runner ran, ran, ran. But no, he couldn't catch up with the hare. So, feeling very abashed, he turned and went back to hell.

'Well, have you brought the princess?' said Satan.

'No, I haven't,' said Swift Runner. 'That gypsy lad is a better man than I am! Why, I couldn't even catch his young brother!' And he told Satan all about it.

'Dunderhead!' yelled Satan. 'That wasn't anybody's young brother, that was a hare!' And he gave Swift Runner a kick that sent him flying to the other end of hell. Then he called his Club Thrower. 'After them, my Club Thrower, and bring me back the princess!'

So Club Thrower set off, and soon overtook Jack and the other two, who were indeed strolling across the plain in no great hurry.

'Come now! Come now!' says Club Thrower. 'Give me back the princess!'

'Give her back to a squinny little chap like you?' says Jack.

'You must prove yourself the better man before we talk of giving things back!'

'Well, then,' says Club Thrower, 'we'll see who can throw my two clubs highest.'

'Right!' says Jack.

So then Club Thrower, who had an iron club in each hand, tossed those clubs so high that they vanished in the clouds.

'I don't call that much of a throw,' says Jack, as the clubs fell to the ground again. And he went to pick up the clubs, took one in each hand, leaned back his head and shouted, 'Hey, brother!'

'What man are you calling with your "hey brother"?' says Club Thrower.

'Oh, just my elder brother, who is a smith on the earth up yonder,' says Jack. 'I'm going to throw the clubs up to him; he could do with some good iron.'

'No, no, gypsy lad, don't do that!' cried Club Thrower. 'I can't lose my clubs. I'd sooner you kept the princess!'

'Oh, very well,' says Jack. 'We'll wish you good morning.'

And he walked away with his father and the princess, and Club Thrower went back to hell.

'Well, have you got the princess?' says Satan to Club Thrower.

'No, I haven't,' says Club Thrower. 'You see it was like this.' And he tells Satan all about it.

'Dunderhead!' screams Satan. And he gives Club Thrower a kick and sends him to join Swift Runner at the other end of hell. Then he calls Whip Cracker to him. 'After them, my Whip Cracker,' says he. 'And don't you dare to come back without the princess!'

So Whip Cracker sets off, and soon catches up with Jack and his party; for they were tired and were sitting to rest outside a little deserted house that had once been a brewery.

'I've come for the princess,' says Whip Cracker.

'Oh, have you?' says Jack. 'You'll have to prove yourself the better man before you can have her. Let's hear you crack that whip of yours!'

So Whip Cracker cracked his whip, and there came a flash of lightning and a clap of thunder that made the ground tremble.

'Pooh!' says Jack. 'Is that all you can do? I can do better than that with a piece of string!' And he took a stick and tied a piece of string to it. 'But first we must make all safe,' says he. And he picked up three barrel hoops that were lying about, and wound one of them very carefully round the princess's head. Then he wound another round his father's head, and the third round his own head.

'What are you doing that for?' asks Whip Cracker.

'Well, you see,' says Jack, 'I'm going to crack so hard, that anyone's head will burst if it hasn't got a hoop round it.'

'Oh, put a hoop round mine too!' says Whip Cracker. 'I've only got one head, and I don't want to lose it!'

So then Jack takes another hoop and begins to wind it tight, tight, *tighter*, round Whip Cracker's head. And Whip Cracker screams out, 'Not so tight! Not so tight!'

'I'll have to wind it tighter yet, if you don't want your head to burst,' says Jack, giving another turn to the hoop.

Then Whip Cracker yells, 'Take it off! I'm going back home – you can keep your princess!'

Jack laughs and takes off the hoop, and Whip Cracker rushes back to hell. 'You can plunge me into ice, or run me through with a three-pronged fork,' says he to Satan, 'but you won't catch me going after that gypsy again!'

So then Satan gives him a kick and sends him to join Swift Runner and Club Thrower at the other end of hell.

'I'll have to go myself,' says he. 'I can't trust these fool servants of mine. But I'm a poor sort of devil if I can't outwit a gypsy!'

So what does he do? He takes four pieces of cloth and two needles, and two reels of thread. And one reel of thread he cuts into small lengths, and the other he keeps whole. And off he goes, and finds Jack and his father and the princess still sitting outside the little house.

'Well, Jack,' says Satan, 'it seems you're not in any hurry to get home.'

'I wouldn't say that,' says Jack, 'only the princess's feet are aching, and my father's not so young as he was.'

'Well, then, I'll tell you what, Jack,' says Satan. 'You're a brave fellow and a clever fellow, and that I'll own. So whilst

your two friends are resting, you and I will have a little contest.
If you win you can keep the princess, and I won't bother you
any more. But if I win then the princess comes back to hell with
me.'

'Fair enough!' says Jack. 'But what is the contest?'

'Oh, just a sewing match,' says Satan.

'Well, I'm not much of a tailor,' says Jack. 'But I'll have to do
the best I can.'

'I've got four pieces of cloth here' says Satan. 'You shall sew
two together, and I'll sew the other two together. And the one
who gets his sewing done first wins.'

'Right!' says Jack. 'And the needles and thread?'

Satan put his hands behind his back. He had one needle and
the reel of thread in one hand, and the other needle and the
short lengths of thread in the other hand. He meant Jack to get
the short lengths, so that he'd be all the time having to stop and
re-thread his needle. 'And it doesn't matter which hand Jack
chooses,' thinks Satan. 'He'll get the short lengths anyway – it's
easy to slip little things from one hand to the other!'

'Right hand or left hand, Jack?' says he.

'Left hand,' says Jack. 'But I think you're cheating!'

'Oh, Jack, Jack, how can you say such a thing?'

'As easy say it as think it,' says Jack.

'Well, you've got the short lengths of thread,' says Satan.
'And that's bad luck for you, Jack.'

'Maybe,' says Jack. 'And maybe not. But the sun out here
dazzles my eyes. So if you've no objections we'll go inside the
house to do our sewing.'

'Inside or out – it's all the same to me,' says Satan. '*My* eyes
are strong enough!' And he snapped his eyes till the sparks flew
out of them.

Well, they went into the house, and Jack led the way into a
very small room; and they sat down at a table under the open
window and began to sew. Jack had to re-thread his needle
every other minute – but what about Satan? Satan's thread was

so long that try as he might, he couldn't find space in that little room to pull it tight; and there he was jumping out of the window between every stitch, yes, and having to run half round the house, too. And Jack laughed so much that he could scarcely see to sew.

'I think you made a mistake there, old boy,' says he to Satan.

'What do you mean?' yells Satan.

'Giving me the short ends,' says Jack. 'And now – here's my pieces of cloth stitched together, so you own up – you're beaten!'

Then Satan gave a scream, threw bits of cloth at Jack's head, took a leap through the window, and rushed back to hell.

Jack and his father and the princess walked on and came to the hollow tree. A hard time they had of it, climbing up through the hollow of that tree! But Jack took the princess on his back, and gave a hand to his father. So, between scrambling and slipping, and clutching and floundering, they got up at last, and came back into the world again.

'And now, my pretty,' says Jack, 'which way to your father's kingdom?'

'I don't know, Jack,' says the princess. 'I was hoping you did.'

'Haven't a notion,' said Jack. 'So we'll just have to walk round the world till we come to it.'

'Oh, Jack,' says the princess, '*more* walking! And me with my legs aching!'

'Well,' says Jack's father, Graf, 'when a gypsy's been living among devils for twenty-two years, and when that gypsy's kept his eyes open, he's learned a thing or two.' And he picked three leaves from a tree and blew on them. What happened? The three leaves turned into three little green horses.

'Now,' says Graf, 'up we get! And you, my little green horses, just you carry us straight to the kingdom of the princess's father.' So the three of them got on to the little green horses, and the little green horses galloped away, and in less than no time brought them to the king's palace. And when they'd dismounted, Graf blew on the little green horses, and they turned back into leaves and floated away. And Jack and Graf and the princess went into the palace.

And when the king saw his only dear daughter returned safe and well, and when he learned what perils Jack had been through to rescue her, he was more than willing to keep his royal promise. That very day he held a wedding for Jack and the princess; and that very day he gave Jack half the kingdom. So here was the gypsy lad, Jack, become a prince, and a happy prince, none happier.

But the old gypsy, Graf, Jack's father, went back to live with his wife and his eleven other sons. Nor, you may be sure, did he go empty handed. He went with enough gold to keep him in comfort for the rest of his life.

5 THE MONKEY NURSEMAID

You must know that in India there were seven brothers who lived in one house. Each of these seven brothers was married, and each of them had one child. So they agreed to hire a boy to look after all seven of the children. 'But he must be a strong lad,' said they, 'because the children are so little that he will have to carry them about.'

Well, a boy came, and he looked strong. But was he as strong as he looked? The seven wives baked a loaf as big as a door, and said to the boy, 'Take it away and eat it.' But the boy couldn't even lift the loaf. So the wives said, '*You* are no use!' And they sent him away.

Now at the top of a tree sat a big monkey. And the monkey had been watching. So when the boy went away, the monkey came down, picked up the loaf, and carried it off, and ate it.

Here indeed was a strong lad! So the seven brothers and their seven wives hired the monkey as their nursemaid, and he used to carry all seven of the children about on his back.

But one day, when the seven mothers were very busy in the house, the children kept rushing in and upsetting things, and the mothers scolded the monkey for not keeping them out of the way. Then the monkey got sulky, and carried the children off to the top of a hill. He didn't bring them back all day. He didn't bring them back when it got dark, either.

The mothers didn't know where the children were, and they were running about looking for them and crying. But the villagers laughed at them, and a woman said, 'Well, what did you expect, engaging a monkey as your nursemaid? As like as not he's gobbling up the children, just as he gobbled up that big loaf!'

'And do you know where the monkey's taken them?' said a man. 'He's taken them to the top of Demon Hill. So if the monkey doesn't eat them, the demon will.'

Oh dear! The mothers spent a miserable night. But they couldn't get any one to go up Demon Hill for them. Nobody dared. They were all too afraid of the demon.

Now as soon as the monkey had carried the children up the hill, he knew how foolish he'd been. But he couldn't carry the children home again, because the demon was prowling round the hill, looking for something to eat. So the monkey carried the children up to the top of a tall palm tree; and when the demon spied them and began to climb the tree, the monkey threw down heavy palm tree fruits on his head, and the demon ran away howling.

But the monkey knew the demon would come back. So he left the children at the top of the tree and ran, ran, faster than fast, to a blacksmith and bought some sharp knives. Then he ran, ran, faster than fast, back to the palm tree, and tied the sharp knives all up the trunk. So when it was night the demon came back and began to climb the tree again. But he couldn't see at all well, for besides its being night, his eyes were swollen up with the bumps the palm tree fruits had given him. So all that happened was that as he climbed he was so badly cut by the knives that he let go his hold and fell to the ground. And there he lay groaning.

'Help! Help! Help!' cried the demon.

Then the monkey swung himself down the palm tree very cautiously, and came to stand beside the demon.

'Help! Help!' cried the demon again. 'I'm dying!'

'Well, I can help you,' said the monkey. 'I can heal your wounds, and I will heal them. But first you must give me some promises.'

'I'll promise anything!' groaned the demon.

'First then, that you won't eat the children.'

'I won't touch them!' sobbed the demon.

'Second, that you will give each of them a set of new clothes, and bring seven little horses for them to ride home on.'

'I'll get all those things as soon as I'm well enough!' cried the demon.

So then the monkey went to gather some healing herbs he knew of, and came back and laid a herb on each of the demon's wounds. And as he laid on the herbs, he was singing a charm:

> '*Whispering, whispering sesamie,*
> *Lonely flowering sesamie,*
> *Tell your grandad, sesamie,*
> *Of seven little pants.*'

That was the first verse of the charm. And the second verse was this:

> '*Whispering, whispering sesamie,*
> *Lonely flowering sesamie,*
> *Tell your grandad, sesamie,*
> *Of seven little coats.*'

And in the next verse it was seven little hats, and in the next it was seven pairs of shoes, and in the next seven little swords, and in the next seven little horses, and in the next it was two big hogs. And in between each verse the monkey blew on the demon's wounds, and the wounds healed up.

'Now get on your legs and be off with you!' said the monkey. And the demon stood up and ran away. The monkey climbed up the palm tree, going carefully to avoid the knives. And when he got to the top he took the seven children in his arms, and they all fell asleep.

At dawn the demon came again, followed by seven little horses and two big hogs. And each little horse had a neat little

bundle on its back. The monkey pulled the knives out of the tree; then he brought down the children, and unpacked the bundles. And in each little bundle was a little pair of pants, a little coat, a little hat, a little pair of shoes, and a little sword. So when he had dressed the children in their new clothes, the monkey lifted each one onto a little horse. Then he and the demon got astride the two big hogs, and the whole lot of them set off merrily for home.

Oh! Oh! When the mothers saw the cavalcade come jingling along, led by the monkey and the demon riding on the two big hogs, they were terrified. But when they saw their children dressed up so fine, each one perched on his little horse, and laughing and calling out to them – why then the mothers laughed and shouted too, for very joy. And since the monkey told them that the demon had promised not to eat anyone, they asked that demon into the house and gave him a splendid dinner. And they gave the monkey as good a one.

But when dinner was over, the monkey stood up and said, 'I'm not going to be a nursemaid any more, because I don't like being scolded.'

And he and the demon rode away on the two big hogs.

6 IRONHEAD

There was a lad called Peter whose mother was dead, and whose father was growing old. So one day the father said, 'My lad, I am getting past work, and it is you now who must earn our bread. Away with you and seek for work; take service with whom you will, only be faithful and always give of your best.'

So off goes Peter. He walks, walks, walks, calling at this house and that house, but nobody seems to want him. The food in his knapsack is all eaten, he is tired and hungry; the sun sets, twilight comes, soon it will be night. What should he do? Should he go home, or should he walk on through the night? He stood and thought.

And as he so stood, he heard the *tap, tap* of a stick, and saw an old man coming towards him. The old man came up close.

'Good evening, sir,' says Peter.

'Good evening,' says the old man. 'And what might you be doing, standing so forlorn on this lonely road with darkness coming on?'

'I have been looking for work,' says Peter. 'But no one wants me.'

'Will you work for me, Peter?'

'Oh gladly, sir, how gladly!'

So the old man took Peter to his house, and Peter served him well and faithfully. It wasn't hard work he had to do: just to tidy up, and cook a bit of food for the old man and himself, and look after two horses and a cow.

And when he had been with the old man for a year, the old man said, 'Peter, you're a good lad, and it's time to talk of wages. Will you have them now, or will you serve me for another year?'

'If I may have my wages,' says Peter, 'I think I should carry them home to my father.'

'Very well, then, very well,' says the old man. And he put a hazel nut into Peter's hand.

Peter looks at the nut, looks at the old man, looks at the nut again.

'Your wages,' says the old man.

'Oh!' says Peter.

'And here's some bread and a bottle of milk to put in your knapsack,' says the old man. 'Now be off home! Goodbye to you, Peter.'

'Goodbye to you, sir.'

And off walks Peter.

A hazel nut! Just one hazel nut to take home to his poor old dad after a year's work! Oh, Peter felt bad about it! And the nearer he got to home, the worse he felt. He sat down in a field to eat his bread and drink his milk: and as he ate and drank he was rolling the nut under his fingers. What was he to say to his old dad? 'Father, I've brought you my wages; Father, I've brought you a hazel nut!' Bah, no, he couldn't take that nut home; he might as well eat it and have done. And he picked up a little stone and brought it down on the nut.

Crack! There lay the nut in two halves.

But – oh, merciful heavens! What was coming out of that nut? Herds of horses, herds of cattle, flocks of sheep, more and more and more, careering all over the place in such numbers that it seemed they must presently fill the whole world!

Up springs Peter, waving his arms, shouting, rushing here, rushing there, trying to collect the careering beasts into an orderly flock that he might drive them home – for oh, oh, oh, what a present for his dad! But the more he shouted and waved his arms, the more wildly the animals stampeded. He was in despair, he was sobbing with vexation and disappointment, when suddenly out of the ground leaped a demon, whose mouth grinned and whose eyes flashed fire.

'Come, come, what's the matter here?' says the demon.

'Matter!' cries Peter. 'Matter enough as you can see for yourself! These are my year's wages, and I'm losing them all!'

'If you'll promise me one little thing, I'll put them all back in the nut for you,' says the demon.

'I'll promise you anything except my soul!' says Peter.

'Bah!' says the demon. 'I don't want your soul. Souls are two a penny, young man – the world's crammed with 'em! All I ask is that you shall never marry.'

'Is that all?' says Peter. 'Yes, I'll promise you that.'

The demon whistled. And at once all the horses and the cattle and the sheep began crowding into the nut again, nearly tumbling over each other in their haste. And when they were all in, the two halves of the nut shell closed together. And the demon picked up the nut and gave it to Peter.

'Crack the nut when you get home,' said the demon. 'And as you crack it you've only to say, "My horses, my cattle, my sheep, the demon Ironhead puts quietness on you," and the animals will become so tame that they'll eat out of your hand ... But remember, I hold you to your promise, my lad!'

Then the demon sank down into the earth; and Peter put the nut into his pocket and walked on home.

His old dad was at the house door, looking out.

'Father! Father! You'll never guess what I've got for you!' And Peter takes the nut out of his pocket.

'My wages!' says he, and laughs.

'Your *wages*?' says his old dad, quite bewildered.

Peter laughs again. 'My horses, my cattle, my sheep, the demon Ironhead puts quietness on you,' says he. And he cracks the nut.

Out come the herds of horses, the herds of cattle, the flocks of sheep, even more of them, it seems, than came out before. But now they stand orderly, filling all the country round the cottage.

The old man gasps and stares. 'Oh, my boy,' says he, 'how did you come by all these?'

So Peter told him the whole story. And the next day they drove some of the flocks and herds to market and sold them for much gold. And with the gold they bought a farmhouse with acres of grassland and a pretty orchard. They still had enough animals left to make them the most prosperous folk in all the neighbourhood. And so they lived in peace and plenty for a time.

But something was troubling Peter's old dad. And one day, as he and Peter were sitting in the orchard, looking out over the fields where their flocks and herds were grazing, the old man said, 'Peter, my son, it's time you married; for I would see my grand-children growing up to enjoy all this wealth before I die.'

'But, Father, I can never marry! Remember the promise I gave to Ironhead!'

'Pooh!' said the old man. 'One promises this, one promises that, but no one can expect you to keep such a promise. It isn't right, nor natural. A man's life is his own to make the best of. Who is Ironhead to say what you must, or mustn't do? Now listen: we'll keep the grey stallion, the swiftest of all our horses saddled night and day. Then if Ironhead should show his ugly face, all you have to do is leap on the stallion's back and gallop off; for that stallion will overtake the swiftest wind that blows; nor can the swiftest wind catch up with him again.'

Well, at first Peter won't hear of it. But his old dad keeps on and on; and truth to tell, there's a pretty girl in the village who has won Peter's heart. So what with his old dad's badgering, and his own wishing, the day came when Peter went courting the pretty girl. And after that it wasn't long before they agreed to get married.

So the wedding bells rang, and the wedding was held, and

the weddng feast was spread, and all the village came to it. And after the feast the tables were put away, the musicians struck up, and every one began to dance. And the music was at its gayest, and the dance at its merriest, when who should look in at the window but the demon Ironhead.

'Hullo, hullo!' says Ironhead. 'What's going on here? It looks to me mighty like a wedding! But am I dreaming now, or was I dreaming then? Wasn't there a promise made . . .?'

Peter didn't wait to hear the end of what Ironhead was saying. Not he! He fled from the room, darted to the stable, leaped onto the grey stallion, and away at a gallop.

Away, away, away, over hill, over dale, through thick forests and wild wildernesses, without stop, without stay, for Ironhead is running fast behind. But Ironhead cannot catch up with that stallion who outruns all winds that blow; and on and on they go, through seven times seven countries, till Peter comes to the house of an old woman, and there he draws rein.

'Mother, mother, shelter me till my stallion gets his breath! For I am fleeing to the world beyond all worlds with Ironhead at my heels!'

'Come in and rest then,' says the old woman. 'You shall have food and drink, and the grey stallion also. I have a little dog who will begin to howl when Ironhead is still seven miles off.'

So Peter went in, and the old woman spread meat and drink before him, and gave the stallion oats and a bucket of water. But Peter and the stallion were scarcely fed and rested when the old woman's little dog began to howl.

'Quick, quick, my son, you must go!' cried the old woman. 'But take this napkin and this cake. Put them in your bag where you can get hold of them easily. Treasure them, treasure them – they may be your salvation!'

Peter took the napkin and the cake, put them in his bag, and calling out his thanks to the old woman, leaped onto the grey stallion, and away at full gallop.

Away, away, away, through seven times seven countries,

through thicker woods and wilder wildernesses, up steeper mountains, down deeper valleys, away, away, away, outracing every wind that blows, till he comes to the world's end, and there he finds the house of another old woman.

'Mother, Mother, hide me, for Ironhead is on my heels!'

'Come in, my son! Rest and eat, you and your grey stallion. I have a little dog who will howl when Ironhead is still seven miles off.'

So Peter went in, and he and the grey stallion were fed and rested. But scarcely had Peter finished his meal, and scarcely had the grey stallion swallowed the last of his oats, when the little dog began to howl.

'Oh, my son, away with you!' cried the old woman. And she also gave Peter a napkin and a cake. And Peter put them in his bag, thanked the old woman, leaped onto the stallion, and rode off faster than the fastest wind that blows.

On and on and on, into the world that is beyond all worlds, with the demon Ironhead racing behind him. Ironhead called to the storm wind, and the storm wind whirled him along; but the grey stallion outraced the storm wind and left Ironhead far behind. So on and on and on, till, at the end of the world that is beyond all worlds, they came to the house of a third old woman.

'Mother, Mother, shelter me till my stallion gets his breath, for Ironhead is at my heels!'

'Come in, my son, you have time to rest and eat, you and your grey stallion. I have a little dog, and he will howl when Ironhead is yet seven miles off.'

So Peter went in, and the old woman gave food and drink to him and the grey stallion. And when her little dog began to howl, and Peter sprang up to go, the old woman gave him a cake and a napkin.

'Listen to me, my son,' said she. 'You have now three cakes and three napkins. Ride for seven days and seven nights straight on; and on the eighth morning you will come to a great fire blazing across your way. Strike the fire three times with the three napkins, and the flames will divide and let you through. And as you pass through you must throw the three cakes behind you with your left hand.'

'Mother, I will follow your counsel in all things.'

'Then haste away, my son, and may heaven protect you!'

Peter sprang onto the grey stallion and galloped on for seven days and seven nights. And with the dawning of the eighth day he came to a wall of fire, so high that its flames touched the clouds, and so broad that there was no way round it. But Peter struck the flames three times with the three napkins, and the flames parted and let him through. And as he passed through, he tossed the three cake behind him with his left hand.

And the three cakes turned into three great dogs, whose names were World's-weight, Iron-strong, and Quick-ear. The dogs came bounding after Peter, baying with joy, and the flames closed behind them: there was the great wall of fire again with no way round it.

And no sooner had the flames closed behind Peter and the dogs than up rushed Ironhead, borne on the storm wind. But the storm wind battered at the flames in vain.

'Ah! Ah! Promise-breaker!' screamed Ironhead. 'You have escaped me this time. But if I have to wait for all eternity, I will catch you yet!'

So Ironhead sat down to wait on one side of the wall of fire, and Peter rode away on the other side. Now he was in no more hurry, and he let the grey stallion take his own pace through a pleasant country till they came to a small white house. And at the door of the small white house, Peter dismounted and knocked.

'Come in!'

Peter went in, and found an old woman spinning, and a beautiful girl sitting at the window combing her golden hair.

'What brings you here, my son, where no man comes?' said the old woman.

'Indeed, Granny, I scarcely know. But I would gladly serve you, if I might.'

'And I would gladly have a servant,' said the old woman, 'to plough and sow my little fields. Is it agreed between us?'

'It is agreed,' said Peter.

So Peter lived with the old woman and her granddaughter, and his life was happy. When he was not working in the fields he went hunting with his three big dogs, bringing home game which the golden-haired girl cooked for their dinner. And Peter grew daily fonder of the golden-haired girl; and the wedding from which he had fled seemed like a dream of long ago – a dream he would willingly forget.

But as Peter grew fonder of the golden-haired girl, so the golden-haired girl grew fonder of him. And Peter said to himself, 'No, this is not right!' So on a day when the grandmother had gone to market, and Peter and the girl were alone together, he told her his whole story. And as the golden-haired girl listened, the tears came into her lovely eyes. But she brushed them away and laughed.

'Can it be true?' she wondered. 'Is it possible that the wall of fire would divide merely at the touch of three napkins? Or is he making up a tale to stop me from loving him? Oh I wish I knew!'

'I must and will know!' thought she. And the next time she was alone in the house (Peter having gone to the fields and her grandmother to market) the girl hurried into Peter's room, snatched the three napkins from the table by the bed, and ran with them all the way to the great wall of fire.

And standing by that wall of fire, she shielded her face with her left hand, held the napkins in her right hand and struck with them against the flame.

She struck once. Nothing happened.

She struck twice. Nothing happened.

But when she struck for the third time the wall of fire parted to right and left – and through the gap between the flames leaped Ironhead.

The terrified girl turned and fled, with Ironhead at her heels. No, he didn't catch her, he didn't want to, but he made her run faster than ever she had run in her life. She reached the little white house, rushed in through the door, and fell in a faint on the kitchen floor. And Ironhead, who had leaped in after her, went to hide himself under the hearthstone.

By and by back from the fields comes Peter, followed by his three dogs. The girl has come a bit to herself, but she looks at Peter with wild eyes, and can only babble about flames and napkins and that terrible, terrible demon! So Peter, thinking he had scared her by his story, lifts her up and carries her to her bed. And thankful he is when her grandmother comes back from market and can see to her.

Next morning the girl was still in a fever, and the grand-mother said, 'I know a herb that would cure her. It has a bright blue flower and grows at the roots of the rowan tree in the little wood beyond the fields. If you will go and pluck it for me, I will seethe it in milk and make her a drink, and we shall soon have her well.'

'I will go this moment,' says Peter, 'but first I will shut up my dogs, lest they bark and disturb our golden-haired girl.'

The grandmother goes upstairs to sit with the girl, and Peter calls his dogs and shuts them up in the stable.

'You must stay very quiet, my dogs,' says he. 'You must not bark, nor whine, nor make any noise at all.'

So the dogs lie down with their heads between their paws, and Peter hurries away across the fields to the little wood.

And when all is quiet in the kitchen, Ironhead comes out from under the hearthstone, and follows after Peter. And isn't he grinning! 'I have you now, you breaker of promises!' he chuckles, as he slips along behind the hedges from field to field and into the wood.

Peter came into the middle of the wood. There was the

rowan tree, and there at its roots was the healing herb with its bright blue flowers. But – what was that? The crack of a twig under somebody's foot! Peter swings round – Ironhead close behind him!

Now Peter is scrambling for his life up into the branches of the rowan tree, and Ironhead is screaming with rage. For the rowan tree is a sacred tree, and nothing evil can touch it. So Ironhead stamps and screams and glares up at Peter with his glittering eyes. And Peter looks down at him from between the branches.

'Come down, come down, you breaker of promises!' screams Ironhead. 'Don't think you can escape me! If I can't climb up, I can wait here to all eternity. But you will hunger and thirst, your head will swim, and you will fall, fall, *fall*, *FALL!* And I shall catch you between my strong arms, and squeeze you to death!'

'Yes, that is true,' says Peter. 'I see that I cannot escape you. And if I am to die, why wait till I hunger and thirst and my head swims? That were to die two deaths instead of one. But before I come down, you must wait until I have called three times.'

'Call away!' mocked Ironhead. 'If you call a hundred times, it will do you no good. For I have you in my power! Ah, I have you in my power!' he shrieked. And he danced in his evil glee.

Then Peter gave a loud shout. 'Iron-strong, World's-weight, Quick-ear, come to my aid!'

And back in the stable Quick-ear lifted his head.

'Listen,' said he, 'our master is calling!'

'Be quiet!' whispered World's-weight, who heard nothing. 'Didn't our master tell us to make no noise?'

'Iron-strong, World's-weight, Quick-ear, come to my aid!' shouted Peter again.

And back in the stable World's-weight lifts his head. 'Quick-ear was right,' says he, 'our master is calling!'

C

But Iron-strong gives World's-weight a cuff with his paw. 'Be ashamed!' he whispered. 'Didn't our master tell us to lie still till he returned?'

And up in the rowan tree Peter began to despair. 'Oh, my dogs, my dogs,' thinks he, 'I am at the point of death, and you won't come to save me!' Then he makes one last mighty effort and calls so loud that the wood rings, 'Iron-strong, World's-weight, Quick-ear, come, come, come! Save me, or I perish!'

And back in the stable Iron-strong lifted his head. 'Yes, now our master is really calling us,' said he. And he sprang at the stable door and burst it open.

Now all three dogs are racing away in the direction of Peter's voice. Into the wood they rush and come to the rowan tree. One glance is enough. '*Gr-gr-gr-gr*, you filthy demon!' Snarling, biting, leaping, tearing, they pounce on Ironhead. And in less than no time they have torn him into little pieces.

Then Peter came down from the rowan tree, and having praised and fondled his three faithful dogs, he plucked the blue flower of the healing herb and went back to the house. The grandmother seethed the blue flowers in milk and gave the golden-haired girl to drink. And the golden-haired girl rose from her bed, as well as she had ever been.

'But oh,' says she to Peter, 'I have done such wrong that I fear you can never forgive me!' And she told him all about the napkins and the parting of the flames, and the coming through of Ironhead.

'If you did wrong, it has turned out right,' says Peter, 'for Ironhead is dead. And now I must leave you, and go home to my wife.'

The golden-haired girl wept, the grandmother wept. Peter was near to weeping himself, but go home he knew he must. And he set out that very day, carrying the three napkins and followed by his three great dogs. But before he went, the girl said, 'I have a ring my godmother gave me. Will you accept it, Peter, and wear it in memory of me?'

'I need no ring to remember you by, for I shall never forget you,' said Peter. But he took the ring and put it on the little finger of his right hand.

Now this ring was a magic ring, but neither Peter nor the girl knew that.

So Peter mounted his grey stallion and rode away, and came to the wall of fire. He touched the fire three times with the three napkins, and the fire parted, and Peter and the dogs passed through. But what was this? As soon as they had passed the fire, the three dogs vanished, and there on the ground where they had stood lay three little cakes. And Peter picked up the cakes and put them in his bag with the three napkins. He came to the houses of the three old women, and to each he returned her napkin and her cake. And from each he received a blessing: and so rode thoughtfully on till he reached home.

Out comes his old dad, shouting a welcome. But where is his wife?

'Oh, my son,' says his old dad, 'your wife believed you dead. And as the marriage was no marriage, she got the law's leave to marry again. Now she has gone with her man into another country.'

Was Peter sorry, was Peter glad? He scarcely knew. He only knew that he felt very lonely; and for half a year he went about his work with a heavy heart. Then one night he dreamed that he took the ring from the little finger of his right hand and put it on the third finger of his left hand. And the dream seemed so real, that when he awoke he did just that.

And then what did he see? He saw the golden-haired girl standing by his bed, and he sprang up and took her in his arms.

'Now you are mine for ever and ever,' says he.

'Yes, now I am yours for ever and ever,' says she.

So they were married, and lived in great peace and happiness all their lives.

Once upon a time what should happen *did* happen; and if it had not happened, this story would never have been told.

Well, there was a man called Karoli with whom nothing prospered. It didn't seem to be his fault, but there it was, he couldn't earn a living anyhow. And at last he decided he'd best hang himself. So off with him to the forest, carrying a long coil of rope, and climbs a tree and fastens his rope to a branch. And a demon who lived in the tree looked out and said, 'Man, oh man, what are you doing with that rope?'

'I'm going to hang myself,' says Karoli.

'Oh,' says the demon, 'I shouldn't do that!'

'What else *can* I do?' says Karoli, 'since I can't earn my bread?'

The demon puts his hand into the tree, brings out two little oxen, the size of peppercorns, and lays them in Karoli's palm. 'Here you are!' says he. 'Treat my little oxen well and they'll make you prosperous. But mind you don't sell them to any one, whatever price you may be offered. And now,' says he, 'be off home with you, and don't you ever come trying to hang yourself in my forest again!'

So Karoli, greatly wondering, carried the two little oxen home.

Next morning, when he woke, there were the two little oxen standing outside his door, yoked to a little wagon.

'Why,' says he, mightily surprised, 'what are you doing with that wagon?'

'Waiting for you to come and fell trees,' said they. 'Hurry now, and bring your axe.'

Karoli fetched his axe and went out. And the peppercorn

oxen set off for the forest so fast that Karoli could scarcely keep up with them. 'Now,' said they, when they got to the forest, 'chop us down the biggest tree you can find.'

Karoli scarce knew whether he was awake or dreaming; but he chopped down a big tree. And when it was down, the two peppercorn oxen drew the little wagon under it. There lay the tree across the wagon, and covering up wagon, oxen and all.

'Chop down another!' cried the peppercorn oxen from under the tree.

So Karoli chopped down another tree, and the peppercorn oxen drew the wagon under it.

Karoli put down his axe and stared, as well he might. But the peppercorn oxen cried out, 'What are you thinking of, Master – loading us up with only two tree trunks? Come, load up the wagon till it groans! We should be ashamed to go through the village with only two trees!'

So Karoli chopped down another great tree, and yet another, and another, and the peppercorn oxen took them all onto the wagon – though how they managed it, neither Karoli, nor you, nor I, nor any one else could ever tell.

But when there were a dozen or more great trees piled up one on top of the other, the wagon gave a groan, and the peppercorn oxen called out, 'Enough! Enough!' and moved off – though there was nothing to be seen of the oxen or of the wagon, only the piled up trees moving along, out of the forest and onto the road.

Well, it so happened that a count, who was Karoli's landlord, was riding along the road with his bailiff. And when the count and the bailiff saw that pile of trees coming towards them, with Karoli walking behind it, they almost fell off their horses with astonishment.

'What's the meaning of this?' cried the count to Karoli. 'How can these trees move of themselves?'

'They are not moving of themselves, most High Born,' says Karoli. 'My little oxen are drawing them.'

The count jumped down from his horse and peered under the trees. And when he saw the two little peppercorn oxen — didn't that count want to possess them!

'How much are you asking for your oxen?' says he.

'They are not for sale, most High Born,' says Karoli.

'Not for sale! And you a poor man who can't earn your bread! Come, I'll give you their weight in silver!'

'They are not for sale, most High Born.'

'Their weight in gold, then!'

'They are not for sale, most High Born.'

The count got angry. He stormed and raved. But Karoli wouldn't part with his peppercorn oxen – no, not for all the gold in the world.

'Obstinate pig! Am I not your landlord?' stormed the count.

'Yes, most High Born.'

'And don't you know that I can turn you out of your house?'

'Yes, most High Born.'

'Then sell me your oxen, if you wish to keep a roof over your head!'

'They are not for sale, most High Born.'

The count wanted to snatch the oxen away from Karoli, but he didn't quite like to do that. So he thought up a plan. 'You see that bleak moor over there, all covered with thorn bushes?' says he. 'That moor belongs to me. If by sundown your oxen can plough up the moor into furrows ready for sowing, you can keep them. If not, I, who am your landlord, will take them from you.'

And off he rides with the bailiff.

Karoli went home sad as sad. He lifted the trees off the wagon and unyoked his peppercorn oxen. There they stood, so tiny, so pretty, creamy white and shining like silk. He didn't want to lose his little oxen, no, he didn't! The tears came into his eyes at the thought of it.

But one of the little oxen up and spoke. 'Don't grieve, dear Master! Only get us something to plough with, and we'll do the rest.'

Then Karoli ran about among his neighbours trying to

borrow a plough. But they laughed at him and said, 'What do *you* want with a plough? You don't possess an inch of ground!' And when Karoli told them he had to plough up the count's moor before sundown, they thought he had gone mad, and bade him take himself off. But at last a farmer said, 'Well, there's a rusty old plough in the corner of my field yonder – you can have that to play with.'

So Karoli picked up his little oxen and carried them to where the plough stood under a wall. Then he set them down and roped them, one in front of the other, to the plough.

My word! The peppercorn oxen set off at a run, drawing the plough behind them, with Karoli at the plough handles and running too. And they didn't stop running till they got to the count's moor. And then one of them said, 'Master, just you lie down there at the edge of the moor and sleep. You can leave the rest to us.'

So Karoli lay down and slept. He slept long – he was worn out with grief and worry. When he woke up – what did he see? The sun drawing to the west, and where the moor had been, a great ploughed field, with furrows straight as ruled lines, and all the thorn bushes cast to one side and blazing in a mighty bonfire.

Karoli ran to tell the count that the work was done. The count called his bailiff; they got on their horses and rode off to where the moor had been. And didn't they stare!

'I've a mind to have you cast on the bonfire for witchcraft!' cried the count.

'Oh most High Born, it is not I but my little oxen who have done the work.'

'Then sell me your little oxen.'

'They are not for sale, most High Born.'

'Stubborn pig that you are!' cried the count. 'Very well then. I have seven big hay fields where the hay is cut and ready for carting. Let us see now what your precious oxen can do! If by sundown tomorrow they can cart all that hay and bring it to my barns, you shall keep them. If not, I will take them from you!'

Karoli lay awake all night, tossing and turning. Now he was sure he was going to lose his little oxen. But early in the morning he heard one of them calling, 'Master! Master!' And when he looked out of the window – there were the peppercorn oxen standing at his door, yoked to their little wagon.

'Time to be stirring, Master,' one of them called. 'We've a long day's work before us. Put your breakfast in your pocket and come along!'

So Karoli put some bread in his pocket and ran out. And no sooner was he outside the door than the little oxen set off for the hay fields, faster than fast.

When they came to the hay fields one of them said, 'Now, Master, we know you've had a bad night. So just you eat your bread and then lie down under the hedge and sleep. You can leave the rest to us.'

Karoli ate his bread and lay down. He was soon asleep. He slept long and long. When he woke, the sun was drawing to the west, and not one swathe of hay could he see in all the seven fields. But on the road beyond the fields stood something that looked like a great golden hill, glittering in the sunlight.

But where were the peppercorn oxen?

'We're here, Master,' called a little voice from under the golden hill. 'Come along!' And the great golden hill began moving off towards the count's castle.

At the castle gates the great golden hill stopped, and Karoli went to call the count.

'Most High Born, I've brought the hay. But if you don't have the castle moved back a bit, we shall have no room for the hay in the courtyard.'

'Insolent wretch!' cried the count. And he bade his servants throw Karoli out. And Karoli fell with a thump into the road.

'Master, dear Master!' cried the little oxen. And they pulled on the wagon – ONE, TWO, THREE! – rushed through the courtyard and brought up against the castle with such a bang that the castle tumbled to the ground, and all the hay fell on top of it.

The count nearly died of rage. He screamed and danced. He called his bailiff, and the two of them ran to unyoke the little oxen. Yes, the count was going to have them this time! If he'd lost his castle, he'd keep the oxen!

But the peppercorn oxen tossed up their little heads, and kicked out with their little heels. And before the count and bailiff could cry 'Oh!' they were both seated in the little wagon. And once seated in that little wagon – can they get out again? No, they can't. They're stuck fast.

Then the little oxen set off at a gallop: they galloped, galloped right across the world, and out of the world, with the count and the bailiff screaming at them to stop. But they didn't stop till they came to hell gate, and at that gate they pulled up with a jerk that sent the count and the bailiff flying headlong out of the wagon and over the gate. And on the other side of the gate the devils caught them on their pitchforks.

The devils had a merry game with the count and the bailiff, playing at catch with their pitchforks. And they enjoyed the game so much that some say they are playing it to this day. But the peppercorn oxen turned the wagon round and went back to Karoli. And they brought the wagon piled up with gold, too. It was the forest demon who gave them the gold as they were passing that way.

So Karoli was rich now, and had no need to think of hanging himself, but lived happily with his little oxen ever after.

Once upon a time there was a blacksmith who had a wife and a great many children. The blacksmith was a good man; he worked hard, he worked well, but he was so poor that sometimes the family was even short of bread, and the children had to go out begging.

Well now, one stormy night, when the wind was howling round the house and the rain sluicing down, and the children were huddled together in their beds trying to keep warm, there came a knock at the door. The blacksmith went to open the door; and who should be standing there but an old man in a tattered cloak, wet through and shivering with cold.

'Shelter! Shelter!' cried the old man. 'Shelter from the wind and rain, and if you can spare it, a morsel of bread!'

'Why, to be sure,' said the blacksmith. 'Come in and welcome. We are but poor folk, as you see, but we'll do what we can.'

Now this old man was the good Golden God with a disguise on him, but of course the blacksmith couldn't know that. All *he* saw was a poor old man. And he brought that old man in, set him before the fire, took off his wet cloak, and wrapped a blanket round him.

'Now,' says the blacksmith, giving the fire a poke and flinging on more logs, 'we'll see what we have in the larder.'

So off he bustles to the larder, and his wife comes behind him and whispers, 'You fool, what are you thinking of? Haven't your children been out this very day begging for bread, and you must go giving hospitality to tramps?'

'Hush, hush, wife!' says the blacksmith. 'It is not only the rich who must show compassion. What have we? Cabbage soup and bread! Well, heat up the soup and be quick about it!'

The wife heated up the soup, but she was all the time scowling and muttering under her breath. Never mind for that! The old beggar ate and drank, and said thank you. Then he lay down by the hearth and fell asleep. And the blacksmith and his wife went to their bed.

Next morning the blacksmith shared his breakfast with the beggar man; and though that breakfast was little enough for one man, it seemed to the blacksmith that it was plenty and to spare for two. And as they ate and drank, the old beggar was smiling at the blacksmith, and the blacksmith was smiling back at him. And it was to the blacksmith as if the world was one big smile. And the more he looked at the old beggar man, the happier he felt.

So, when they had finished breakfast, the old beggar man got up to go. He took his staff in his hand and said, 'Do you know who I am?'

'I've been having a good guess all through breakfast,' said the blacksmith. 'And if you are whom I think you to be, will you please to bless me before you go?'

And down he knelt at the beggar man's feet.

The beggar man took the blacksmith by the hand and raised him up. 'You have my blessing,' says he. 'And you shall have something else. You shall have three wishes, and your wishes shall come true. Think carefully before you speak, that you may not waste your wishes.'

'No need to think,' whispered the blacksmith's wife, giving her husband a nudge. 'Ask for riches!'

'Hush, woman,' said the blacksmith. 'Leave me to think.'

And he stood and thought, and his wife kept nudging him and whispering, 'Ask for riches, you fool, ask for riches!'

'Yes,' said the blacksmith at last. 'That's it! I have an old wooden armchair here. I would wish that whoever sits in that chair may not be able to get up without my permission.'

'Your wish is granted,' said the good Golden God. And he smiled. 'Now for your second wish,' said he.

Again the blacksmith stood and thought. And again his wife kept nudging him. 'Are you mad?' says she. 'Ask for riches, you fool!'

'I shall ask for what I think best,' said the blacksmith. And after he had thought a bit longer he said, 'I have an apple tree growing in my garden. The tree bears good fruit, but mostly that fruit is stolen from us by the neighbours. I would wish that whoever climbs up into that tree shall not be able to come down again without my permission.'

'Your wish is granted,' said the good Golden God. And he laughed.

'Are you gone clean crazy?' screamed the blacksmith's wife. 'Letting a fortune slip between your fingers! If you'd asked for riches – wouldn't you have been able to buy apples and everything else we need?'

'It is up to me to wish,' said the blacksmith. 'I shall ask for what suits me.' And he stood and thought for long enough. And all the time he was thinking, the good Golden God was smiling, and the blacksmith's wife was clamouring, 'You have only one more wish! Ask for riches, you fool, ask for riches!'

So after he had done thinking, the blacksmith took from his pocket an old purse shaped like a little bag, with the mouth tied up with a thin leather thong. The purse was empty.

'Ah, now you're coming to your senses!' cried his wife. 'Ask that the purse may be always full of gold!'

But the blacksmith said, 'I wish that whatever goes into this purse shall never come out again without my permission.'

'You have your wish,' said the good Golden God. 'And you have my blessing along with it. And now good day,' says he, and off he goes, chuckling to himself.

All that day, and for many days afterwards, the blacksmith's wife was scolding and shedding tears. Well, it did seem hard, poor soul – her husband having the chance of a fortune and throwing it away like that! The man must be crazy! And to be poor, and to have a crazy fool for a husband, was enough to make any woman shed tears! So her tears fell and her tongue clattered. But the blacksmith didn't take much notice; he worked all day in his forge.

Well, maybe a week later, there comes a stranger to the forge. He's a tall dark man, grandly dressed, with a conceited smirk on his face.

'Good morning, blacksmith,' says the tall dark man.

'Good morning to you,' says the blacksmith.

'I have come to ask you a question,' says the tall dark man.

'Ask away,' says the blacksmith.

'Someone told me that you had a visitor a week ago,' says the tall dark man.

'Someone hasn't lied then,' says the blacksmith.

'Well, then,' says the tall dark man, 'what did your visitor give you?'

'Nothing,' says the blacksmith. 'And I asked for nothing.'

'Nothing, nothing, nothing! You surprise me! You took him in, warmed and fed him, and he gave you nothing? What ingratitude! Now I am a very different sort of person. I don't ask for kindnesses before giving rewards. From this moment I can make you very rich and very happy and very comfortable. Do you know who I am?'

'I've been having a good guess,' says the blacksmith. 'Are you by any chance the devil himself?'

'The devil himself,' says the tall dark man with a conceited smirk. 'Now what do you say? Shall I give you gold, shall I give you silver, shall I arrange that you have but to put your hand in your pocket to draw out all the money you can desire, not once, or twice, but at all times?'

'And what do you ask in return?' says the blacksmith.

'Oh, the merest trifle,' says the devil. 'And nothing for the present. Only that in ten years' time you shall come with me to hell and be my servant.'

'If you can get me there,' says the blacksmith.

'Oh, I'll get you there all right,' says the devil.

'Done!' says the blacksmith.

'Done!' says the devil. 'And to prove I'm a man of my word, just put your hand in your pocket.'

The blacksmith put his hand in his pocket. Sure enough his pocket was full of gold coins. 'Yes,' says he. 'I grant you're a fellow of your word.'

'See you again then in ten years,' says the devil.

And when he'd said that, he vanished.

So, from then on, the blacksmith had only to put his hand in his pocket to pull out all the money he could ever spend. Yes, he was very rich, and very happy, and very comfortable. He spent and spent, and what he couldn't spend he gave away to anyone in need. His wife and his children were happy too. His wife didn't weep and scold any more; she dressed herself up and flaunted about like any duchess. The children, too, had pretty clothes and the best of good food. And all went merrily for five years. And then one morning, when the blacksmith was alone in the house, the door flew open, and there was the devil.

'Time's up!' says he.

'Now how can that be?' says the blacksmith. 'You gave me ten years, and but five have passed.'

'Five years of days and five years of nights makes ten,' says the devil. 'Come along.'

'But I'm enjoying myself so much,' says the blacksmith. 'And you're not playing fair. I must have another five years!'

'No, no,' says the devil, 'you must come now.'

'Well, if I must, I must,' says the blacksmith. 'But if we've a long way to go, I'd best put on my boots, for these slippers aren't meant for walking in.'

'Then get your boots,' says the devil. 'Only hurry up. I can't wait all day.'

'Shan't be a jiff,' says the blacksmith. 'I'll just run upstairs for the boots. And meantime do take a seat.' And he pushed forward the old armchair.

The devil sat down; the blacksmith went upstairs. Very soon he came down again with his boots on.

'Ready?' says the devil.

'Quite ready,' says the blacksmith.

'Well, then, let's be off,' says the devil. And he made to get up.

What's this? He can't get up. He's stuck to that old armchair as if he was glued there.

'Gone a bit stiff?' says the blacksmith. 'Here, let me help you up!' And he fetched a stout oak cudgel and began to beat the devil with it. *Whack, whack, whack!* 'Up with you! What, can't get up? What's happened to your legs then?' *Whack, whack, whack!* Harder and harder, till he has the devil bellowing like a bull. *Whack, whack, whack!* 'Now will you get up? Now, I say!'

'I can't get up!' bellows the devil.

'Strange!' says the blacksmith. 'Perhaps another stick might help?' And he fetches another stout cudgel, and it's *whack, whack, whack,* with a cudgel in each hand, and all the strength of his brawny muscles behind them.

It wasn't long before the devil was roaring for mercy. So, after a little more beating, the blacksmith said, 'Will you promise me ten more years?'

'Yes, yes!' howls the devil.

'And gold in my pocket as before?'

'Yes, yes!' screams the devil.

'Then you may get up and be off with you,' says the blacksmith. And the devil leaped out of the chair and fled away in a flash.

So for ten more years the blacksmith lived richly and happily. And then one day in autumn he was standing in the doorway of his forge when he saw, far off but coming rapidly nearer, a dark cloud that looked like a big swarm of bees.

'Ha!' says he to himself, 'this looks like visitors!' And he stepped into his forge, took a long iron bar with a spiked end, thrust that spiked end into the forge fire, and blew up the fire with the bellows. And every now and then he went to look out of the door. The dark cloud was coming nearer. It was like an immense flock of black birds now.

The blacksmith ran to his forge and worked the bellows again. The spiked end of the iron bar was now glowing red. So again to the door to look out. The huge dark cloud was quite near. Black birds indeed! Not a flock of black birds but the devil himself, with a whole crowd of little devilkins swarming behind him.

And now here stood the devil at the door of the forge.

'Sorry to interrupt your work,' says he, 'but time's up. And you see I've brought my people with me. No armchair for any of us this time! Come! Hurry!'

'Oh no, oh no!' cries the blacksmith. 'Not now, when I'm so happy! Do give me just a few more years!'

'Not I!' says the devil.

'Just one more year then!' pleaded the blacksmith.

'Certainly not,' says the devil.

'Just a week then!'

'No!'

'Well, just one more day! Only one more day!'

'Not another minute,' says the devil.

The blacksmith heaved a great sigh and rubbed his fist across his eyes. 'Well, if I must, I must! But you see I'm in my working clothes. I shouldn't like to disgrace you in hell, and you dressed up so fine! I'll just change into my Sunday suit, and then I'll be with you.'

'Oh, all right,' says the devil. 'Only hurry up.'

Now all this time the little devilkins were jostling and pushing and crowding round the forge door. And the blacksmith said, 'How can I push my way through all this crowd? Do you boys like apples?'

'Yes, yes, yes!' shrilled all the devilkins.

'Well then, there's an apple tree in the garden. You just go and help yourselves . . . The apples won't be any more use to me now,' says he with a sigh.

So off rushed the devilkins and swarmed up into the apple tree. The devil stood under the tree, waiting for the blacksmith to change into his Sunday suit. Soon the devilkins were munching happily. 'Oh,' cried they, 'these are the sweetest apples ever we tasted!'

'Throw me down a big one,' says the devil.

'No, no!' cried the devilkins. 'Climb up and choose one for yourself!'

So the devil climbs up into the tree.

And when the blacksmith saw that the devil and all the devilkins were safely up in the tree, he darted back into his forge, snatched up his iron bar with its red hot spike, and came out at a run. 'How do you like my apples? How do you like my apples?' cried he, prodding and poking at first one and then another of the devils in the tree. Backs, haunches, hands, feet – they all got stabs from the sharp point of that red hot spike, till they were screaming with fright and pain, and the devil's coat tails were ablaze.

'How do you like my apples? How do you like my apples?' laughed the blacksmith. 'Howl away up there, devil and devilkins! You can't come down till I give the word. And I shan't give the word until you promise me another ten years of freedom, with as much gold in my pocket as before.'

'I promise! I promise!' screamed the devil.

Then the blacksmith said 'Come down.' And down they all came, and rushed off wailing.

Another ten years passed. The blacksmith was still happy and contented, enjoying his riches, and giving away money to all in need. So that the people said, 'There never was as good a man on earth as our good blacksmith!' But the ten years came to an end. And one morning, when the blacksmith opened the door – there was the devil, and with him a swarm of devilkins, blue and green and red and yellow, a huge crowd of them, surrounding the house on all sides.

'Ho! Ho!' says the blacksmith. 'Is this all of you? Haven't you left just one or two at home?'

'Not I!' said the devil. 'I'm making sure of you this time, you cunning scoundrel. Come along. Time's up! You don't trick me again!'

'I don't know that I want to trick you,' said the blacksmith. 'I've had a good life, but I'm getting a bit tired of it. Anything for a change, you know … All the same, you startled me appearing all of a sudden in such numbers – as if you'd risen out of the ground! How did you manage it? I begin to think you must be even more powerful than the good Golden God himself!'

'Ha!' said the devil with a smirk. 'We mayn't have *more* power, but we certainly have *some*! For instance, we can make ourselves invisible; we can go in and out without being seen; we can take any shape we please; we can make ourselves large, we can make ourselves small . . .'

'It's all very fine to boast,' said the blacksmith, taking his purse from his pocket. 'But when the good Golden God so pleases, he can make himself and his people so small, so small, that they can all get into this purse. Do you mean to tell me that you and *your* people, horns, tails, and all, could do as much?'

'Nothing easier,' smirked the devil. 'We should change ourselves into smoke.'

'I shan't believe it till I see it,' said the blacksmith. He untied the leather thong from the neck of his purse, and held the purse open between his hands. 'Now, boaster, let's see you do it!'

Pssst! The devil blows through his teeth, devil and devilkins disappear, a trail of grey smoke curls round and round the room; and steadily, steadily the smoke drifts into the purse till not a trace of it remains outside.

And the devil calls from inside the purse, 'Well, are we all in? Or are we not in?'

'You are in,' said the blacksmith. And he drew the thong tight round the neck of the purse. 'Now it's my turn to show what I can do,' says he. And he lays the purse on his anvil, takes up his heavy hammer and beats, beats, beats.

The devils shouted, the devils screamed, the devils shrieked. The smithy rang with all the noises of hell. And above the din sounded the steady beat of the blacksmith's hammer, ker-*flump*, ker-*flump*, ker-*flump*!

'Let us out! Let us out!' screamed devil and devilkins.
Ker-*flump*! Ker-*flump*! Ker-*flump*! went the hammer.
'Have you had enough?' shouted the blacksmith.
'Oh! Oh! Oh! Enough and too much!'
'Rubbish that you are,' shouted the blacksmith. 'I will flatten you all to farthings if you don't promise me to go away and never come back.'

'I promise!' howled the devil. Then the blacksmith untied the neck of the purse and out rushed devil and devilkins, blue, green, red and yellow, squealing like pigs. They darkened the earth, they darkened the sky, such crowds of them as there were. But the darkness rushed farther and farther away, till it vanished behind the horizon, and the kindly sun shone out of a clear sky onto the blacksmith standing at the door of his forge.

'Phew!' said the blacksmith, wiping the sweat from his face. 'That was a near go! But even the devil must keep his promises.'

And he went into breakfast with a good appetite.

Once upon a time a little boy and a little girl, Jan and Jeanette, went into the forest to pick wild strawberries. But the sky grew dark, thunder growled, lightning flashed. Jan and Jeanette ran; they lost their way, and when the storm had ceased it was night.

How to find the way home? The children didn't know. And there were wolves in the forest – they could hear them howling.

Said Jeanette to Jan, 'Little brother, climb up this tree. Perhaps you will see a light shining from some house where we might shelter.'

So Jan climbed up the tree; and Jeanette stood under the tree and called, 'Do you see anything, little brother?'

And Jan answered, 'No, little sister – only the spreading boughs of this tall tree above me.'

And Jeanette called, 'Climb higher!'

So Jan climbed higher. And Jeanette called again, 'Do you see anything now, little brother?'

'No, little sister; only the dark branches of the forest.'

'Climb higher, climb higher!' called Jeanette.

So Jan climbed to the very top of the tree, and Jeanette called, 'Do you see anything now, little brother?'

'Yes, little sister; now I see a house with a lighted window.'

Then Jan came down from the tree, and the children went on through the forest to the house.

Knock! knock! knock!

The door opened, and a big woman, holding a lighted candle, looked out.

'Well, I never!' says she. 'Here's a couple of shrimps!'

Says Jan, 'We got lost in the forest.'

Says Jeanette, 'We are afraid of the wolves. Please shelter us!'

'I don't know about shelter,' said the big woman. 'My master is a demon, and he eats little children. Would you rather be eaten raw by wolves, or eaten cooked by a demon?'

Then Jeanette began to cry, and the big woman said, 'Well, come your ways in. You shall have a warm, and a sup of milk and a bite of bread. But stay you can't, for in one hour my master will come home.'

So she brought the children in to the fire, and gave them some milk and some bread. There was a big clock over the mantelpiece. The clock was going *tick-tock, tick-tock*. And the woman was watching the clock.

Tick-tock, tick-tock: the minute hand was going round. *Tick-tock,* fifteen minutes passed. *Tick-tock,* half an hour passed. *Tick-tock,* three-quarters of an hour passed. The children were feeling warm and cosy, when the big woman shouted, 'Now go!'

And she pushed the children out of the house.

It was dark outside. The children were frightened. 'Let us stay! Please let us stay!'

'Can't be done,' said the big woman. 'But stop snivelling, do! We'll see if we can hide you.' And she took the children round to the back of the house where there was a hollow tree. 'Up with you!' says she, and helped them up into the hollow of the tree. 'Crouch down and keep still as mice. If you rustle, if you sneeze, if you so much as twitch an eyelid – it's all over with you!'

The children crouched down, clinging to one another. And the woman went back into the house.

Tick-tock, tick-tock ... Clang, clang, clang, clang ... The huge clock struck the hour. In rushed the demon, snuffling and roaring, '*Norr! Norr! Norr!* I smell man's flesh!'

'Fiddle-de-dee!' said the big woman. 'You and your nose! I've roasted a calf for your supper. Come and eat.'

The demon sat down and ate. For a while he's pleased, he grins and smacks his lips. Then he begins sniffing again. '*Norr! Norr! Norr!* I do smell man's flesh, I *do!*'

'There's no flesh here but calf's flesh,' says the big woman. 'And that's now inside you. Stop your nonsense – lie down and sleep.'

But the demon wouldn't lie down and sleep. He was running about the room and sniffing. '*Norr! Norr! Norr!* Man's flesh, I tell you, man's flesh!'

He looked under the table, he looked under the bed, he looked in all the cupboards, he looked inside the clock case, he searched the whole house, sniffing and sniffing. And then he opened the back door, and stepped out into the garden. '*Norr! Norr! Norr!* I can smell it! I can smell it!'

'Of course you can smell it, you old nuisance,' says the big woman. 'But it isn't man's flesh. It's the insides of the calf I threw out and haven't buried yet.'

'Man's flesh, I tell you! Man's flesh!' *Sniff, sniff, sniff*, all round the garden till he came to the hollow tree. '*Man's flesh!*' he screamed. And he put his hand into the tree and dragged out the children.

'Ah ha! A roast for tomorrow! And for tonight – into the cellar you go!'

And he locked up the children in the cellar, where all night long they sat and wept.

In the morning the demon was in a wonderfully good temper. All through breakfast he's grinning and chuckling. 'We'll have a better supper today than yesterday,' says he to the big woman. 'But we'll hang 'em a bit before we cook 'em, for hanging makes tender.' And he took two ropes, made a noose in each of them, carried the ropes up into the cock-loft, and hung them over a beam. Then he went to fetch the children.

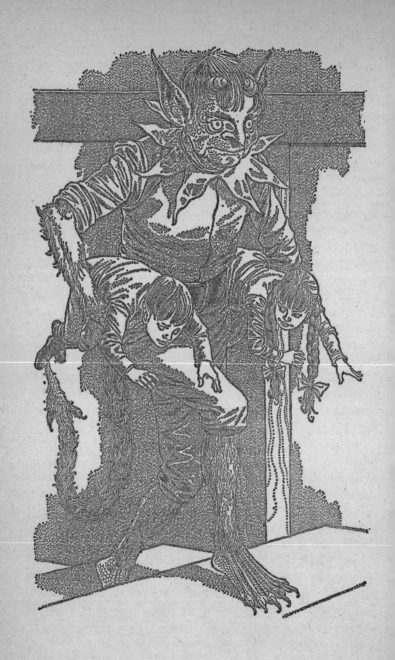

'Ah, my tender chicks,' says he, carrying them, one under each arm, up into the loft. 'See here's a nice long ladder, and up there are two pretty little nooses. So up with you, and just put your pretty little heads into the two pretty little nooses. One at a time, one at a time, of course, since we've only one ladder. And ladies first,' says he, pouncing on Jeanette.

'Oh, little brother, little brother, what shall I do?' whispered Jeanette.

'Be brave, little sister,' whispered Jan. 'Be brave, and very, very stupid.'

Jeanette climbed slowly up the ladder. When she got to the top she took the noose in her hand, swung it, twisted it, bumped her head against it, twisted it some more. Now she had that noose all tangled.

'Put your head into it!' screams the demon.

'I don't know how to,' says Jeanette, twirling the noose round and round.

'Must I come up and show you?' yells the demon.

'Yes, please,' says Jeanette.

She came down the ladder, and the demon climbed up. 'You do it like this,' says he. 'It's easy as . . .'

But Jan pulls away the ladder. And there's the demon hanging.

The demon roared, the demon choked, the demon turned black in the face. 'Let me down! Let me down!' he splutters.

'No,' says Jan. 'You can hang.'

'I'll give you anything you ask!' gasps the demon.

'And you won't eat us?' says Jan.

'No! No! No!'

'And what will you give us if we let you down?'

> *'I'll give you, I'll give you*
> *My red horse, and my white horse,*
> *I'll give you, I'll give you*

My kittel-kittel car,
Laden with gold and silver!'

said the demon.

'Well, then,' says Jan, 'you can come down.' And he set the ladder against the beam, climbed up, and untied the noose from round the demon's neck.

The demon felt very ill. He thought he would now kill both the children. Then he thought better of it. He was a bit afraid of them. His head was splitting and his hands were shaking: he didn't seem to have strength enough to kill a fly. So he staggered away into the stable, and brought out his little red horse and his little white horse.

'I'll saddle them for you and you can ride off,' says he.

'No,' says Jan, 'that wasn't all you promised us.'

So the demon went into the coach house and brought out his kittel-kittel car, which was a little ivory chariot with four wheels.

'Get in and be off!' he screamed. 'Get in and be off!'

'No,' says Jan, 'that wasn't all you promised us.'

'Oh! Oh! Oh!' the demon shrieked. But he ran into the house, came out again carrying two sacks, one full of gold, and one full of silver; and he tossed the sacks into the kittel-kittel car.

'And may you get lost, get lost, get lost!' he screamed. 'May you never come to your journey's end!'

But the children laughed, jumped into the kittel-kittel car, and drove off.

The demon went and lay down on his bed. 'I'm dying!' he groaned. But the big woman made him a posset, and he drank it up and fell asleep.

When he woke he thought what a fool he'd been. 'I wasn't in my right mind,' said he. 'I should have killed those children! And now we've nothing for supper ... Ha! But I can catch them yet!' he shouted. And he jumped out of bed and ran off after the children.

The little red horse was galloping, galloping. The little white horse was galloping, galloping. Jan cracked a little whip, Jeanette clapped her hands; the kittel-kittel car was bouncing along right merrily.

The children had come out of the forest now. They were driving down a sandy road among fields, and they came to a man hoeing potatoes. Jan threw the man a piece of gold and called, 'If someone comes along and asks you:

> *Have you seen pass*
> *Jan and Jeanette,*
> *And my red horse, and my white horse,*
> *And my kittel-kittel car,*
> *Laden with gold and silver?*

you must say, "No, I haven't seen them." Don't forget!'

The man picked up the piece of gold and shouted, 'No, I won't forget.'

So they drove a little farther and came to a man hoeing turnips. Jeanette threw him two pieces of gold and called, 'If someone should come along and ask you:

> *Have you seen pass*
> *Jan and Jeanette,*
> *And my red horse, and my white horse,*
> *And my kittel-kittel car,*
> *Laden with gold and silver?*

you must say, "No, I haven't seen them." Don't forget!'

'I won't forget,' shouted the man, picking up the two pieces of gold.

So on they go in the kittel-kittel car, with the red horse galloping, and the white horse galloping, till they come to a man

picking apples in an orchard. Jan throws the man three pieces of gold, and shouts, 'If someone comes along and asks you:

> *Have you seen pass,*
> *Jan and Jeanette,*
> *And my red horse, and my white horse,*
> *And my kittel-kittel car,*
> *Laden with gold and silver?*

well, you haven't seen them. Don't forget!'

'I won't forget,' says the man, picking up the three gold pieces.

So the children drive on. But now comes the demon, *flip, flip, flip*, racing on his long legs. He sees the man hoeing potatoes, and shouts:

> *'Have you seen pass*
> *Jan and Jeanette,*
> *And my red horse, and my white horse,*
> *And my kittel-kittel car,*
> *Laden with gold and silver?'*

And the man answers, 'It will be two years before the potatoes are ready.'

'Fool!' screams the demon. 'I wasn't speaking of potatoes!'

'I told you – not for two years,' says the man.

And that's all he would say, however much the demon raged and swore.

So the demon raced on. He came to the man hoeing turnips and shouted:

> *'Have you seen pass,*
> *Jan and Jeanette,*
> *My red horse, and my white horse,*
> *And my kittel-kittel car,*
> *Laden with gold and silver?'*

And the man answered, 'It will be two years before the turnips are ready.'

'Fool, fool, fool!' screams the demon. 'I wasn't talking about turnips!'

'But I was,' says the man.

So then the demon threw a clod of earth at the man, and raced on, *flip, flip, flip,* his long legs bounding, his long feet leaping, and comes to the man picking apples in an orchard.

'Hey, you!' screams the demon,

> *'Have you seen pass,*
> *Jan and Jeanette,*
> *My red horse, and my white horse,*

> *And my kittel-kittel car,*
> *Laden with gold and silver?*

answer me, knave, and if you talk about apples I'll dash your
brains out!'

So then the man was frightened and said. 'Yes, I saw them.
They went that way.' And he pointed down a by-road that led
to a river.

The children *had* gone that way, and now they could hear
the demon, *flip, flip, flip,* coming down the road behind them.
They came to the river bank, and there were ten women washing linen. 'Oh, hide us! Hide us!' cried the children. 'The
demon is close on our heels!'

Now there were some thick bushes growing near the river,
and the women bade the children drive in among the bushes.
Then they spread the washed sheets over the bushes. The sheets
covered the bushes down to the ground; you couldn't see the
children, nor the little red horse, nor the little white horse, nor
the little kittel-kittel car.

Up comes the demon and yells out:

> '*Have you seen pass*
> *Jan and Jeanette,*
> *My red horse, and my white horse,*
> *And my kittel-kittel car,*
> *Laden with gold and silver?*'

'Oh yes, sir,' says one of the women, 'we saw them.'

'Then where are they now?' roared the demon, And he
began to sniff the air. '*Nor! Norr! Norr!* I can smell 'em! I can
smell 'em!'

'Very like you can,' says the woman. 'They have but just now
gone across the river, and the wind's blowing this way.'

'But how did they get across?' shrieked the demon.

'In one of our big linen baskets,' says the woman.

'Then I'll cross the same way!' yelled the demon.

There were several empty linen baskets standing on the river bank, waiting to be filled with the clean washing. The demon pounced on the largest of the baskets, pushed it into the water, jumped into it, and away with him across the river, paddling with his hands. But when he got to the middle of the river, the current caught the basket and swirled it round and round. The demon paddled with all his might, but the current was stronger than he was. The current carried the basket away and away. It tossed it here, it tossed it there, it tossed the demon out into the water. And there he was, swimming, swimming, till he came to a whirlpool. And the whirlpool sucked him down . . . and down . . . and down . . .

Then the washerwomen took the sheets off the bushes and said to the children, 'Come out! The demon is drowned, and you can now go home.'

'But which way *is* home?' says Jan.

'Follow the road by the river bank and you'll come there,' said the women.

So Jan stood up in the kittel-kittel car and cracked his whip. And Jeanette stood up in the kittel-kittel car and clapped her hands. The little red horse galloped, the little white horse galloped, the kittel-kittel car bounced merrily along. And Jan called out, 'Catch!' and Jeanette called out, 'Catch!' And there they were, tossing out gold and silver along the river bank for the women to pick up.

But though they threw out a lot, they had more than a lot left. And that more than a lot they brought home and gave to their father and mother.

In a faraway kingdom there was a palace which was hung with mourning, and a king and a queen who always dressed in black: a palace where nobody laughed, where the courtiers walked on tiptoe, and a glad, loud voice was never heard. And why was this? It was because the king's son and daughter had been stolen away, and none knew where to find them.

Now one day there came to the palace a lad seeking service. The lad was handsome and clever and good; and when he was offered a job as messenger boy, he said, 'That's the very work for me! For I'm light and quick on my feet, and I like looking about me.'

The lad was sent into all sorts of strange places, seeking for the prince and princess; and though he never found them, he was so ready and faithful in all that he did that he rose in the king's favour. The king dressed him in a rich suit of black, and consulted him about this, that, and the other thing. As to the queen, it seemed to her almost as if she had been sent a second son in the place of the one she had lost.

But the king's steward became fiercely jealous of the lad, and determined to get rid of him. He thought and thought of how he could do this, and one day he hit upon a plan.

Now you must know that the king had once lent the devil some money, and the devil refused to pay it back. So one day the steward went to the king and said, 'That messenger boy of yours is a big boaster.'

'Is he?' said the king. 'I hadn't noticed it.'

'He boasts that you and the queen both love him,' said the steward.

'Well, so we do,' says the king.

'Ah, but he boasts that he knows the way to hell. And that he could easily go there and get your money back from the devil.'

'That would be very convenient for me,' said the king. And he sent for the lad.

'I hear you know the way to hell,' says the king to the lad.

'Oh no, your majesty, not I!' says the lad.

'And I hear that you said you would not be afraid to go there and get back the money the devil owes me.'

'Your majesty,' cried the lad, 'I never said any such thing!'

'But if you haven't said it,' went on the king, 'how could the story have got about?'

'That I cannot say, but I can guess,' said the lad. And he tossed up his head and walked off proudly.

All that day the king kept looking at the lad in a puzzled kind of way; and the lad's pride was stung to think that the king should doubt his word. So next morning he went to the king and said, 'I *don't* know the way to hell, but if you wish I will go there.'

'And get my money back?' said the king.

'And get your money back,' said the lad, very stiff and proud.

'It must be a long way,' said the king. 'I don't ask you to walk there.'

'I will walk, or run, or ride, according to your pleasure,' said the lad.

'Then go to the stable, and take any horse you fancy,' said the king.

The lad went to the stable. He didn't feel very happy. He looked at one horse, and he looked at another horse. And there was a billy goat in a corner of the stable, and the billy goat said, 'Better take me. I know the way.'

So the lad got onto the billy goat's back, and rode off.

Now when it was known that the lad had set out for hell, the jealous steward rejoiced. But the queen hurried to the king and said, 'Isn't it enough that we have lost our son and daughter, but you must send this lad to his death also?'

Then the king was ashamed of what he had done, and he sent mounted messengers galloping after the lad to fetch him back. But the lad said, 'I obey the first command of the king, and not the second.' And he bade the messengers go home, and rode on into the wide world, by whichever way the billy goat chose to take him.

The billy goat trotted along the high road; and at first it was light and open, and then it was dark and shut in. For the high road passed through a great forest. And on one of the forest trees sat a raven.

Says the raven to the lad, 'Whither away?'

Says the lad to the raven, 'To hell, to get the king's money back from the devil.'

Says the raven, 'That's a long journey and a dangerous one. Dig under the roots of this tree and you'll find a sword. It's a magic sword, and everything you strike with it will burst into a thousand pieces.'

'That's a sword worth having!' said the lad. And he dug under the tree, found the sword, picked it up, and slung it from his belt.

'And now,' says the raven, 'a piece of advice. Never turn aside from the highway.'

'That sounds good counsel,' said the lad. 'I'll remember it.'

Then he said goodbye to the raven and rode on, and the raven was croaking after him from the top of the tree. '*Pawk! Pawk!* If you reach hell gate you'll find my sister there. Greet her from her brother in the forest. But hold the highway! Don't turn aside! *Pawk! Pawk!* Hold the highway as you value your life!'

And he went on calling after the lad, till the lad was out of earshot.

By and by, still keeping to the high road, the lad and the billy goat came out of the forest into open country. And they hadn't gone far before the lad saw a hideous old woman, seated on a nanny goat, come galloping towards him out of a by-road.

'Hi! Hi!' called the old woman. 'Stop a minute!'

So the lad pulled up the billy goat and waited.

'Good day, my handsome,' says the old woman, galloping up to him. 'And where might you be going?'

'To hell,' says the lad. 'To ask the devil for the money the king lent him.'

'And aren't you making a long journey of it!' says the old woman. 'It'll take you all your life to get to hell the road you're going. Just you follow me, and I'll show you a short cut.'

Pawk! Pawk! The raven's voice seemed to be still echoing in the lad's ears. *Hold the highway as you value your life!* 'Thank you kindly, old mother,' says the lad, 'but I'm sticking to the road I'm on.'

'You're a fool!' cried the old woman. And she gave the nanny goat a cut with her switch, and galloped away in front of the lad till she came to another by-road. And down that by-road she turned and disappeared from sight.

'Do you know who that was?' says the billy goat.

'Not I,' said the lad.

'That was the devil's grandmother,' says the billy goat.

'Then we're well quit of her,' says the lad.

The high road was going up a steep hill now. At the top of the hill was a little walled town. The gates of the town were shut fast, and on one of them hung a silver trumpet. Before the gates sat twelve maidens, weeping bitterly.

'Why do you weep?' said the lad, reining up the billy goat.

'We weep because a monster comes to eat us for his supper,' sobbed one of the maidens.

'That's bad!' said the boy. 'And what's this for?' says he, taking down the silver trumpet from the gate.

'Oh, don't blow it! Don't blow it!' shrieked all the maidens together. 'That trumpet holds our life-span, for the sound of it will summon the monster. In one hour a herald will come to the gate and sound the trumpet. Don't rob us of our last hour!'

'But I've a mind to see that monster,' says the lad. And he puts the trumpet to his lips and blows a loud blast.

The trumpet gave forth a sound that rang over hill and valley. And there, flapping up the hill, half-running, half-flying, came a winged monster with twelve heads. The monster's twelve jaws were snapping, and his twenty-four eyes were shooting out sparks of fire. When he saw the lad he let out such a roar that the whole world echoed. But the lad had his sword drawn; he touched the monster with it, and the monster burst into a thousand pieces.

Then the city gates flew open, the maidens ran in; all the bells in the city began to ring, and the people came out, dancing and shouting.

'Stay with us, stay with us, you shall be our king!' they cried to the lad.

But the lad said, 'No, I ride on.'

And he trotted away on the billy goat.

The high road now went down into a valley. It was a broad white ribbon, stretching on and on, across open country. And out from a side turning galloped the hideous old woman on her nanny goat. 'You'll never reach hell the way you're going!' says she to the lad. 'Come now, follow me, I can show you a short cut.'

But again the lad said he was sticking to the high road, and the old woman called him a fool, and galloped away in front of him, till she turned down another by-road, and disappeared.

'You've done well so far,' said the billy goat. And he trotted on till they came to another steep hill. Up that hill they went, still following the high road, and came to the top where there was another walled town. The gates of the town were shut fast; from one of the gates hung a silver whistle; and in front of the gates sat twenty-four maidens, weeping bitterly.

'Why do you weep so bitterly?' said the lad.

'Oh, oh, oh, because a monster with twenty-four heads comes to eat us for his supper.'

'And will this whistle summon the monster?' says the lad, taking the silver whistle from the gate.

'Don't blow it! Don't blow it!' shrieked the maidens. 'Spare us our last hour of life!'

'But I want to meet that monster,' said the lad. And he put the whistle to his lips and blew a long shrill note that rang over half the world.

Then up the hill came a monster with twenty-four heads, and twenty-four legs and twelve wings. The monster's twenty-four jaws were snapping, and his forty-eight eyes shot out sparks of fire. When he saw the lad he let out such a roar that the hill trembled and the valley shook, and far, far away hell's gate shuddered. But the lad touched the monster with his sword, and the monster burst into a thousand pieces.

The city gates flew open, the twenty-four maidens ran in; all the bells in the city rang; out came the people, dancing and shouting.

'Stay with us, stay with us, you shall be our king!' they cried.

But the lad said, 'No, I ride on.'

And he trotted away on the billy goat.

So down once more into a valley. And once more out from a by-road comes the hideous old woman, the devil's grand-mother. The old woman is hot with rage and hatred, but she grins and tries to look pleasant.

'Your little billy goat is half-dead with weariness,' says she. 'But my little nanny goat is fresh and lively as a lark. Come, we'll change mounts!'

'No thank you, Mother,' says the lad.

'Shall I show you a short cut then?' says she.

'No thank you, Mother. I hold the highway.'

'You stubborn fool!' shrieks the old woman. 'I'll make you

rue it! *I'll make you rue it! I'LL MAKE YOU RUE IT!*'

And off she galloped, screaming and lashing the nanny goat, till she turned down a by-road, and vanished.

'There's temper for you!' says the billy goat. 'But there's a reason for it.'

'And what is the reason, my billy goat?'

'Oh, you'll find out soon enough,' says the billy goat. And on he trots till they come to the top of another hill, and there's another walled city with locked gates. On one of the gates hangs a silver bugle, and in front of the gates sit thirty-six maidens, weeping bitterly.

'Then I take it there's a monster coming to gobble you all up?' says the lad, lifting down the bugle from the gate. 'Now I mean to see that monster,' says he. And he puts the bugle to his lips.

'Don't blow it! Don't blow it!' shriek the maidens. 'Spare us our last hour of life!'

But the lad blows a blast that echoes throughout the world. The monster comes. He has thirty-six heads, and eighteen wings; his seventy-two eyes shoot out flames, and every one of his thirty-six mouths is wide open, ready to gobble up a maiden. But the lad touches him with his sword, and the monster bursts into a thousand pieces.

The city gates open, the maidens run in, the bells ring, the people come out, dancing and cheering. Now they would have the lad stay to be king over them, but the lad says, 'No, I ride on.' And ride on he does, down the other side of the hill, and hasn't ridden much farther before he comes to hell gate.

The lad remembers the raven's words, 'If you reach hell gate you'll find my sister there. Greet her from her brother in the forest.' But all he sees, coiled about hell gate, is a huge and hideous serpent. The lad looks at the serpent; the serpent looks at the lad. The serpent has friendly eyes.

'Well, I don't know if I'm doing the right thing,' says the lad, 'but I was given a message for someone at hell gate. And the message was, "The brother in the forest greets his sister".'

Then the serpent uncoiled itself from the gate; the gate opened, and the lad rode through.

Then came the devil rushing to meet him, and shouting, 'Get out! What do you want? Get out! What do you want?'

'I come for the money you owe the king,' says the lad.

'You shan't have it!' says the devil.

But up came the hideous old woman, the devil's grandmother, and whispered in the devil's ear, 'Get rid of that lad, quickly, quickly. He is a sly and dangerous fellow! He has killed my three children, my three darling monsters. He holds a sword that can burst all hell into a thousand pieces!'

So then the devil becomes very polite. He puts the king's money in a bag, and hands it to the lad. 'With my compliments, sir,' says he. 'And I wish you a pleasant journey home.'

The lad took the bag, the devil gave a bow, his grandmother gave a curtsy, the lad rode out through hell gate, and there was the great serpent stretched along the ground. It looked at the lad with friendly eyes, and said, 'Please pull off my skin.'

'That would take some doing!' said the lad.

'Please!' said the serpent. 'Please, please, *please*!' And the tears brimmed up in its friendly eyes.

So the lad jumped off the billy goat, and grasped the serpent's skin in his two hands. He pulled, pulled, pulled from the tail to the head. He pulled so hard that the skin came off, and the lad fell down with a jerk. When he stood up again, the serpent had gone. And who should stand there in its place but a lovely princess.

'Oh!' said the lad. 'Oh!'

The princess laughed. 'Take me back to the king and queen,' said she, 'for I am their daughter. And my brother is the raven in the forest.'

The lad set the princess up behind him on the billy goat, and the billy goat scampered off. 'We must make what haste we can,' says the billy goat. 'For I think we shall be followed.'

And sure enough, they hadn't gone very far when they heard

the *pat, pat, pat* of galloping feet behind them. The lad looked round – what did he see? The devil and his grandmother, seated on the nanny goat, and tearing along the road behind them.

The billy goat gallops, the nanny goat gallops; the nanny goat is gaining on the billy goat. But the princess turned her head and spat on the road; and there now, between the billy goat and the nanny goat, lay a great lake.

Off the nanny goat jumped the devil. Off the nanny goat jumped the grandmother. They both knelt, put their mouths to the lake, and began to drink. *Gulp, gulp, gulp* – they drank that lake dry, and up on the nanny goat's back once more, and coming on again.

The billy goat gallops, the nanny goat gallops; the nanny goat is gaining on the billy goat. But the princess takes a glass bead from her pocket and throws it behind her. And there now, between the billy goat and the nanny goat, rises a glass mountain.

So the devil leaves his grandmother sitting under the glass mountain, and away with him back to hell to get the nanny goat fitted out with spiked shoes. And when she had been fitted with spiked shoes, the nanny goat carried the devil and his grandmother up over the glass mountain and down onto the road again.

The billy goat gallops, the nanny goat gallops. The nanny goat is gaining on the billy goat. The nanny goat is so close now that the billy goat can feel the devil's hot breath on his tail. But the princess cries out, 'Light before! Darkness behind!'

And behind the billy goat rises a thick, black fog, though all in front is clear and shining.

So, in that thick black fog, the devil and his grandmother and the nanny goat wandered here, wandered there, and found the darkness ever around them. But the billy goat and the lad and the princess rode on in clear shining daylight till they came to the great forest.

And on one of the forest trees sat the raven.

'*Pawk! Pawk!*' says the raven, flying down from the tree. 'Welcome, my sister, welcome, my lad, welcome, my good little billy goat! Now, my lad, take your knife, cut off my head, and put it on again back to front.'

'Oh no, my raven!'

But the princess said, 'Do as my brother tells you.'

So the lad, little willing, cut off the raven's head, and set it on again, back to front. The lad shut his eyes after that, not bearing to see what he had done. But he heard the princess laughing, he heard a man laughing, so he opened his eyes. What did he see? No raven, but a handsome dark-haired prince, holding the princess by the hand.

'Now we will all go home,' said the princess.

And go home they did, joyously, joyously, the princess riding on the billy goat, and the lad and the prince walking at her side. By the time they reached the king's palace it was night, and the doors of the palace were locked. The lad put the billy goat back in the stable, and took the prince and princess up to his own room, which was in the loft over the stable. The prince and the princess lay down in the lad's bed, the lad lay on the floor, and they all fell asleep.

And in the palace the queen woke from her sleep and shook the king by the arm.

'Wake, wake!' cried she. 'I dreamed that the lad had come back, bringing our stolen children!'

'Let me sleep,' said the king. 'Why wake me for a dream?'

So the king slept again, and the queen slept again. And again the queen dreamed, and again she woke the king.

'I have dreamed the same dream again!' she cried. 'I dreamed that the lad had come, bringing our stolen children, and that the billy goat was back in the stable.'

'Alas, alas, dreams go by contraries,' said the king. 'Let me sleep; for only in sleep can I forget our stolen children.'

So the king slept and the queen slept. And again the queen dreamed, and again the queen woke, and again she woke the king.

'I have dreamed the same dream three times,' said she. 'I am going to see if the billy goat is back in the stable. And if you won't come with me, I shall go alone.'

But of course the king would go with her! They both hurried to the stable. And there was the billy goat.

'Oh billy goat, good billy goat,' cried the queen, 'where is the lad?'

'Look upstairs,' says the billy goat.

The king and queen went up the ladder to the loft. What did they see? They saw the lad stretched on the floor, they saw the prince and princess lying on the lad's bed, and all three sleeping peacefully.

The king laughed and shouted, the queen laughed and cried, the three sleepers woke. There was hugging and kissing and shaking of hands, and a running back into the palace to spread the good tidings. The palace was stripped of its mourning and decked with flowers. The king and queen cast off their black garments and arrayed themselves in crimson and gold. The jealous steward was banished; the lad married the princess; the prince got half the kingdom.

And so we will take our leave of them. For if sorrow began the story, joy has ended it. And may we all live happily!

11 THE LITTLE RED MANNIKIN

There were two brothers; one was rich, one was poor. Krok was the name of the rich brother, and Janko was the name of the poor brother. Krok owned a farm, and Janko worked on the farm. Sometimes Krok paid Janko a few pence; but most often he only gave him his food, and not too much of that. For Krok was very mean, and he said that a morsel of food and a copper or two was all Janko was worth.

So one day Krok said to Janko, 'Tomorrow morning we will go into the forest to cut wood. And see you come early and don't keep me waiting.'

Next morning Janko rose at dawn, and went to Krok's house. But Krok was still snoring in his bed, and Krok's wife said, 'I'm not going to wake him; you'll have to go alone, Janko. And here's something for your breakfast,' said she. And she gave him a little piece of bread.

Janko took the bread, shouldered his axe, and set off alone. And as he went along he was sighing. 'Oh, what a little piece of bread for the whole day!' So, though he was very hungry, he only ate part of the bread. And when he got into the forest, he put the rest of the bread into his jacket pocket, took off the jacket, and laid it on a tree stump. Then he began to cut down wood.

All the time he was working he was thinking about that bread, and getting hungrier and hungrier. But he said to himself, 'No, I won't eat it yet; I must wait a little longer.'

And so he went on working. But as one hour passed, and another hour passed, the moment came when he felt he couldn't wait another minute, and he threw down his axe and ran to take the bread out of his jacket pocket.

But – oh me! – what's this? The pocket is empty, the bread has gone!

Janko almost shed tears, and he almost cursed the thief. But then he said, 'Well, poor devil, whoever he is, perhaps he was even hungrier than I am!' And no sooner were the words out of his mouth than a tiny red mannikin leaped from behind a tree.

And in the tiny red mannikin's hand was Janko's piece of bread.

'Here you are!' says the mannikin, holding out the bread, 'Since you haven't cursed me, I'm giving it you back. I'm not all that hungry myself. Come, eat up!'

So Janko ate up the bread, and the red mannikin watched him and laughed.

'Will you take me into service?' says the red mannikin, when Janko had swallowed the last crumb.

'*I* take you into service!' says Janko. 'How can I? I haven't enough food for myself!'

'Never mind for that,' says the mannikin. 'I can find my own food.'

'But I haven't a penny to pay you wages!' says Janko.

'Never mind for that,' says the mannikin. 'I'll work without wages.'

'It's daft!' says Janko.

'No, it ain't,' says the mannikin. And he kept on and on bothering Janko to take him into service, till at last Janko had to agree.

'Well, then, now to work!' says the mannikin. He seized Janko's axe, and with one stroke of that axe he felled a whole tree.

Janko stood and stared. In no time the mannikin had that tree chopped into faggots, and the faggots corded into neat bundles. And he and Janko between them carried the bundles back to Krok's house.

Then the mannikin waited outside the gate, and Janko carried the bundles of wood into one of Krok's big barns. Krok came out wiping his mouth – he had but just finished breakfast. 'I shan't want you any more today,' says he to Janko.

'If I could have something to eat?' says Janko.

'Didn't my wife give you some bread?' says Krok.

'She gave me a little piece,' says Janko.

'Well, then, take yourself off,' says Krok, 'before I kick you out!' So Janko went sadly away.

The red mannikin was still waiting outside the gate.

'Did you get anything to eat, Master?' says the mannikin.

'No,' says Janko.

'Well, never mind, I'll go threshing,' says the mannikin. And he leaps over the gate and runs into Krok's house.

'Do you want a thresher?' says the mannikin to Krok.

'I could do with one,' says Krok. 'But I want a sizeable one, not a midget.'

'Give me a trial,' says the mannikin; 'you can't think how strong I am!'

'Very well,' says Krok. And he laughs. 'But mind you, I don't give wages for nothing.'

'I don't expect that,' says the mannikin.

So Krok laughs again, and takes the mannikin into a huge barn that was heaped up with piles of wheat, and piles of rye, and piles of barley.

'I'll leave you to it,' laughs Krok, and goes away.

Well, Krok hadn't been gone five minutes, when the mannikin puts his head out of the barn and calls, 'Hi!'

'What now?' shouts Krok.

'I've finished,' said the mannikin.

'I don't believe it,' shouted Krok.

'Seeing's believing,' says the mannikin. 'Come and look.'

So Krok went back to the barn. And sure enough, all the threshing was done.

'I don't know who you are, or what you are,' says Krok. 'But

I'll own you're quick, and I'll own you're strong. And now, what do you want in payment?'

'Oh, just a little corn,' says the mannikin.

'Well, take as much as you can carry,' says Krok. ('And that won't be much!' thinks he.) 'But if you want corn you must go and find a sack.'

The mannikin went out. In a meadow at the side of the house there's a maid spreading linen to bleach in the sun. But there's a wind blowing, and the linen is flapping about. One corner up, one corner down, and billowing here, and twirling there. The maid can't get it to lie smoothly. 'Oh, the devil take the linen!' says she.

'Thank you very much,' says the little red mannikin. And he gathers up all the linen in his two little arms and carries it away.

Then he sat down by a brook where there were rushes growing. And he picked the rushes. And so, with the rushes for thread, and a thorn for a needle, he sewed all the linen together into one enormous sack.

So back with him to the barn to fill the sack. And when he had filled it – my word! There wasn't a grain of wheat, or of barley, or of rye left in all that big barn – only the piles of husks lying.

The mannikin swung the full sack onto his shoulders. Now you couldn't see the mannikin: only the enormous sack and two little red feet sticking out below it. So *trit trot* with those little feet out of the barn, and past a dairy where a maid was churning butter. The maid was hot, the maid was tired. 'Oh, the devil take the butter!' says she.

'Thank you very much!' says the mannikin. He stretched out his little hand and swung the churn, butter and all, up on top of the sack.

Then *trit trot, trit trot* on his two little feet, out of the dairy and round the corner of Krok's house. Krok was having his dinner.

'I'm off now!' shouts the mannikin.

Krok looked out of the window. He couldn't see the mannikin. All he could see was a sack as big as a haystack, with a
churn on top of it, moving away down the road. So in puzzle-
ment he hurried to the barn. What did he see there? Only husks

lying. 'Thief! Thief! Thief!' he screamed. And he ran to the stable, led out his big stallion, jumped onto the stallion's back and galloped off after the mannikin. But no sooner did the stallion sniff the mannikin than he reared up on his hind legs, and Krok fell off.

'Oh, the devil take the stallion!' yelled Krok.

'Thank you very much,' says the mannikin. And he put out a little hand and lifted the stallion onto the top of the churn. Then away with him again, *trit trot, trit trot*; and going like the wind.

Krok was raging. He went to a field where he kept a savage bull, opened the gate and drove out the bull. 'After him, my bull!' he cried. 'After that monstrous thing that's moving down the road!'

The bull didn't need telling twice: he bellowed, put down his head, and charged after the mannikin. But when the bull came close, the mannikin put out a little hand and lifted the bull up on top of the stallion. Then away with him, *trit trot, trit trot*, and going like the wind, till he came to Janko's poor little house.

At the house door he set down the bull and the stallion. What did he do with them? He turned them into two little chips of wood and put them in his pocket. Then he carried the churn and the huge sack into Janko's kitchen.

'Master,' says he, 'here's corn and here's butter. So cook and eat.'

Janko was so hungry that he didn't stop to ask where the mannikin had got these things from; he set to work and baked some flat cakes, and he and the mannikin sat down to supper.

But in the morning Krok went to the judge to complain that Janko had stolen all his corn and all his linen and his churnful of butter. And the maid who had been bleaching the linen, and the maid who had been churning the butter, went with him. The judge sent for Janko and Janko came, with the little red mannikin trit-trotting beside him.

'Why did you take all Krok's corn, and why did you take his linen and his butter?' said the judge to Janko. 'Have you anything to say for yourself?'

'No, he hasn't,' said the little red mannikin. 'Because he didn't take those things. *I* did. And I was within my rights. Krok said, "Take as much corn as you can carry," and that's all I did take. As for the two maids, one said, "The devil take the linen," and the other said, "The devil take the churn and the butter." AND I AM THE DEVIL,' says he. 'And if you doubt it, keep your eyes open, for seeing's believing.'

The little red mannikin drew in a big, big breath, and puffed it slowly out again. And as he was puffing out that breath so he was growing. He grew bigger, and *bigger*, and *BIGGER*. His head touched the ceiling, and his head went through the ceiling, and there were flames darting out of him in all directions. The judge crept under the table, Krok and the maids took to their heels, and Janko stood with his mouth open, staring.

'Goodbye, my friend,' cried the devil to Janko.

Then he gave a leap, and the whole of him went through the ceiling and vanished.

The judge crawled out from under the table. 'I will have nothing more to do with this business,' says the judge to Janko. 'You can keep the corn and the other things, but you'd best go home.'

So Janko went home. He sold the corn and bought land and cattle. Now he was as well off as his brother Krok.

Krok found his stallion back in the stable, and his bull back in the field: he couldn't bear the sight of them, and he sold them to Janko. He was raging with jealousy. 'You'll come to a bad end,' said he to Janko. '*I* wouldn't stoop so low as to have dealings with the devil!'

However, Janko didn't come to a bad end. He lived happily. But he never saw the little red mannikin again.

Once upon a time there was a poor widow who lived with her three daughters in a lonely cottage among the hills. Now this widow had a hen who laid her an egg every morning, and the widow prized that hen greatly. But one day – mercy me! – the hen was missing. The widow searched here, searched there – no, she couldn't find that hen. So she said to her eldest daughter, 'Go out and look for the hen. For have it back we must, even if the silly creature's gone and got itself inside one of the hills.'

Well, the girl goes off, searching here, searching there, and calling *Chuck, chuck, chuck, chuck, chuck!* But not a sight of that hen could she get. And she's just about to turn round and go back home, when she hears a voice speaking out of a cleft in a rock:

> *'Your hen trips inside the hill,*
> *Your hen trips inside the hill.'*

So she runs to a cleft in the rock to scramble down inside it. But the rock gives way under her, and she tumbles through a trap door, down, down, down into a vault under the hill. And still she hears the voice calling:

> *'Your hen trips inside the hill,*
> *Your hen trips inside the hill.'*

'Well,' thinks the girl, 'here I am inside the hill, but where can that hen be?' And she goes through a door out of the vault and comes into a grand room. She goes through this grand room, and comes into another one. She goes, goes, through one grand room after another, and all the time she's calling, *chuck, chuck, chuck, chuck, chuck,* and the voice is answering her:

> *'Your hen trips inside the hill,*
> *Your hen trips inside the hill.'*

Only she didn't find that hen. But in the last room she came into, she found something else: and that was a demon.

'Good morning, my pretty one,' says the demon, grinning and flapping his long ears. 'Will you marry me?'

'No,' says the girl, 'I will not.'

'Then why did you come here?' says the demon. And he struck her dead, and flung her into the cellar.

Well, since the girl didn't come home, the widow said to her second daughter, 'Off with you now, and see what's happened to that sister of yours. And have a good look round for the hen at the same time.'

The second sister goes off, searches here, searches there, and all the time calling, 'Sister! Sister! Sister!' And *Chuck, chuck, chuck, chuck, chuck!* But not a sight of her sister or of the hen does she get. So she's just about to turn and go back, when she hears that voice calling:

> *'Your sister trips inside the hill,*
> *With the hen she trips inside the hill.'*

And the voice is coming from the cleft in the rock. So she runs to that cleft and peers down, and it happens to her just as it had happened to her sister. She loses her footing and falls, comes to the vault, goes out of the vault into one grand room after another, and in the last room – there's the demon.

The demon's grinning and flapping his long ears.

'Good morning, my beauty. Will you marry me?'

'Marry you!' says she. 'Certainly not! I'm looking for my

sister and my mother's hen. And if you've got them, you must give them back to me.'

Then the demon strikes her dead, and flings her into the cellar.

So, when neither of the girls come home, nor was anything seen of the hen, the widow was sobbing and lamenting. And the youngest daughter said, 'Don't fret, little Mother, I'll find them!'

And off she goes.

She searches here, searches there, and all the time she's calling, 'Sisters! Sisters! Sisters!' and *Chuck, chuck, chuck, chuck, chuck!* But she doesn't find her sisters and she doesn't find the hen. And she comes to the cleft in the rock and hears the voice:

> *'Your hen trips inside the hill,*
> *Your sisters trip inside the hill.'*

Then it happened to this girl just as it had happened to her sisters: she peered down into the cleft of the rock, missed her footing, fell into the vault, and went from one grand room into another.

But the demon wasn't in any of the rooms, not even in the last one: he was just coming up from the cellar. And the cellar door was open, and the girl peeped in. What did she see? Oh me! She saw her sisters lying dead.

The demon shuts the cellar door behind him. He's grinning and flapping his long ears.

'Good morning, little lovely one! Will you marry me?'

'That I will!' says the girl.

So then the demon grins more than ever, and makes such a breeze with the flapping of his long ears that the girl's blown backward against the door.

'Now you shall have everything you want, everything!' shrieks the demon. And he dressed the girl up in fine clothes and treated her like a queen.

The girl puts up with him for some time, but every moment she's thinking about her mother and her sisters. So one day she acts very miserable, sighing and snuffling; and when the demon asks her why she's grieving she says, 'I'm sorrowing for my poor mother. She has now no one to work for her, and how do I know she isn't starving?'

'Well you can't go home,' says the demon. 'I shan't let you. But if you like to put some food in a sack, I'll carry it to your mother.'

'Oh, how good of you!' cried the girl.

The demon went to get on his boots, and the girl got a sack and some food. But into the bottom of the sack she stuffed all the gold and silver she could lay hands on, and that was a lot. Then she put some bread and meat on top of the gold, and tied up the sack with a strong cord.

'Here you are,' says she, when the demon came back with his boots on. 'But you mustn't look in the sack. You mustn't even untie the cord, because a present must only be opened by the one it's meant for.'

'I won't untie the sack,' says the demon.

'Well, see you don't,' says the girl, 'because I shall be watching you!'

So the demon sets off with the sack, and the girl goes up to the cleft in the rock and looks after him.

But what with all the gold and silver in it, the sack was very heavy, and the demon hadn't gone far before his back began to ache. And he plumped himself down and said, 'The old body can't want all this food!' He was just about to untie the cord and empty out some food from the sack, when the girl called from the cleft in the rock, 'I see you! I see you!'

'Dear me!' says the demon. 'What sharp eyes my wife's got!'

And he shouldered the sack again and walked on.

When he came to the widow's house, he heaved the sack in through the front door and shouted, 'There's food for thee from thy youngest daughter, and she wants for nothing!'

Then he went back to the hill.

And it happened that there was a goat browsing on the hill, and when the goat saw the demon coming it was frightened, and gave a jump and fell down the cleft of the rock into the vault. So when the demon came in and saw the goat there, he was furious and roared out, 'Who sent for thee, thou long-bearded beast?' And he struck the goat dead and flung it into the cellar.

The girl sees him and begins to cry. 'I would have liked that goat for a pet!' she sobs.

'Well,' says the demon, 'you needn't pull a long face about that! I can soon put life in the creature again.' And he takes down a flask that hangs on the wall, and rubs the goat's eyes and nose and mouth with an oil that's in the flask. And the goat leaps up, alive and frisky.

'Ha!' thinks the girl. 'That flask's worth something!'

Now the demon would often go off to visit his brother demons who lived in the other hills that were scattered here and there about the country, and often he would be away for quite a long time. So one day, when he had gone to a hill that was a long way off, the girl took down the flask of oil from the wall, ran to the cellar where her dead sisters were lying, and anointed the eyes, nose, and mouth of her eldest sister with oil from the flask.

And her eldest sister rose up alive and laughing.

'I'm going to put you in a sack,' says the girl to her eldest sister. And she told her sister what she must do if the demon tried to open the sack.

So, when the demon came home again, there was the sack waiting ready, with the eldest sister curled up inside it, and some bread and meat tucked on top of her.

The demon was in a good temper – laughing and flapping his ears.

'What, another sack full of food?' says he.

'Yes,' says the girl. 'And do, please, please take it home to my mother. I'm sure by this time she must be hungering again. And the thoughts of how hungry she must be makes me want to cry.'

'Oh, you shan't cry,' says the demon. And he heaves the sack over his shoulder.

'But promise me not to undo the cord,' says the girl. 'Remember what I told you about a present.'

'Oh no, I won't undo it!' says the demon.

'You'd better not,' says the girl, 'because I shall be watching you.'

So the demon set off with the sack. And if the first sack had been heavy, this sack was heavier. He had to keep stopping to get his breath. But every time he stops, the girl calls from the cleft of the rock, 'I see you! I see you!' And on he trudges again.

By and by the path took a bend round a field with a high wall, and the cleft in the rock was hidden. So the demon sits down under the wall and says, 'She can't see me here. So I'll just open the sack and throw out some of the food.' And he's about to untie the cord, when the girl that's in the sack calls out, 'I see you! I see you!'

'Whoever would have thought it!' says the demon. 'What eyes my wife has in her head! She can even see through a stone wall!'

And he gets up, shoulders the sack, and trudges on to the widow's house. He doesn't even wait to throw the sack in through the door; he just heaves it down on the threshold, shouts out, 'Here's some more food for thee from thy daughter!' and off with him back to the hill as fast as his aching limbs will let him.

Well, as you may guess, it wasn't long before the girl did the same thing with her second sister. The very next time the demon went to visit his relations, she brought her second sister to life by rubbing her with oil from the flask, put her in a sack with a great heap of gold and silver round her, and just a little food on top, and tied up the mouth of the sack with a cord.

'I'm sure my mother must be hungering again by this time,' she said to the demon when he came home. 'So please carry this sack of food to her.'

'Oh, I don't want to!' groaned the demon. 'Your sacks make my back ache!'

'Well, then, I'll carry it myself, if you'll let me.'

'No, no, you shan't do that. You've got to stay where you are!' said the demon. And he heaved the sack over his shoulder and set off.

'But don't you dare to open the sack!' the girl called after him. 'I shall be watching you!'

Well, the demon plods along and plods along; and if the other sacks had been heavy, this one's heavier. So, when he gets behind the wall, he sits down to rest, and his fingers are playing with the cord at the mouth of the sack. He badly wants to untie that cord, but he daren't.

'What a mistake it is to marry a wench who can see through stone walls!' he sighs. And he gets up and plods on.

His back ached, his legs ached, his neck ached, he was one ache all over. So, when he came to a place where the bushes grew high and thick, he plunged in among the bushes and sat down for another rest. 'And I *will* open the sack and throw some of the food away,' says he, 'because *nobody* can see me here!' But just as he was about to untie the cord from the mouth of the sack, the second sister called from inside the sack, 'I see you!'

'Oh, what eyes she has, what eyes!' moaned the demon. And he got up in a fright and walked on with the sack across his shoulders, and never stopped again till he came to the widow's door.

'Here's some food for thee from thy daughter, who's well and wants for nothing!' shouts he. And he lays down the sack on the doorstep, and off with him back to the hill.

The girl had his supper waiting for him. She was laughing. 'Well, was my mother pleased?' says she.

'I didn't stop to find out,' says the demon. 'But I'll tell you one thing, I'm not going to carry any more of your food sacks!'

'I shan't ask you to carry any more,' says the girl. 'My mother will have enough food now to last her till doomsday.' And she laughs again.

But the next morning she wrapped up her head in a big scarf and told the demon she was feeling very ill. 'I don't know what's come over me,' says she. 'I've a pain in my head and a pain in my stomach. I'll just have to lie down all day. I can't cook you any dinner.'

'Then I'll go and visit my uncle,' says the demon. 'He keeps a good table. But you'll have a bite of supper waiting for me when I come home, won't you?'

'I can't say,' answered the girl. 'May be yes, may be no.'

'You'd better,' says the demon. 'I don't like sick wives.'

And off he goes to visit his uncle.

Soon as he's gone, the girl jumps up, takes off her dress, and stuffs it with straw. Then she takes the scarf from her head, wraps it round a bundle of straw, and sets it on top of her stuffed out dress. Now she has a straw dummy of herself.

Next she puts a cauldron of soup on the fire, leans the straw dummy against the chimney corner with a ladle sticking out of one sleeve, so that it looks for all the world as if it's leaning over the cauldron to stir the soup. And having done all this, she climbs out through the cleft in the rock, and runs home in her petticoat.

The goat was browsing on the hill, and when he saw the girl running away, he called out, 'Wait for me!' and ran after her. So they both reached the widow's house at the same time, and in with them, and slammed the door.

In the evening, home comes the demon, and sees the dummy in the girl's dress leaning over the fire. 'So you're well again!'

says he. 'And the soup smells good. Come on now, serve it up!
I'm hungry!'

Well, of course, the dummy doesn't move.

'Didn't you hear me?' says the demon. 'I said "Serve up the
soup!"'

But the dummy doesn't move.

So then the demon thinks it's the scarf round the girl's head
that's making her deaf, and he screams, 'Take that rag off your
head!'

And still the dummy doesn't move.

So then the demon gets angry, and makes a snatch at the
scarf. What does he find under the scarf? A head of straw! And
what does he see now leaning up against the chimney corner? A
straw dummy!

The demon let out such a yell that the hill trembled. He
leaped out from the cleft in the rock, and raced off after the girl.
But when he got to the widow's house the door was bolted, and
the billy goat was standing outside it.

The demon went to bang on the door, but the billy goat put
down his head and gave that demon such a butt in the stomach
that he tumbled backwards. He got to his feet with a roar, and
the three sisters looked out of an upstairs window. They were
laughing. So he went to bang on the door again. But the billy
goat butted him in the stomach, and the three sisters went on
laughing. And what with the sisters laughing at him, and the
billy goat butting him again and again and tumbling him off his
feet, the demon felt so ashamed that he ran away. He didn't go
back to the hill, either – he ran right out of the country.

So after that the widow and the three girls lived happily,
with plenty of gold and silver to spend. As to the hen, she came
walking in one morning as calmly as if she'd never been away.
But where she'd been all this time she wouldn't say. And so I
can't tell you.

ALLSORTS – 1
Edited by Ann Thwaite   25p

All sorts of things for all sorts of children under
ten.

'Perfect for rainy days' – HOMES AND GARDENS
'A box of delights' – THE FINANCIAL TIMES
'Should guarantee some quiet times for grown-
ups' – TEACHER'S WORLD

ALLSORTS – 2
Edited by Ann Thwaite   25p

The second helping of a delightful treat.

'A choice collection' – DAILY MIRROR
'Not only easy, absorbing, delicious (like trifle),
but good' – THE OBSERVER
'First class' – BOOKS AND BOOKMEN

Lewis Carroll

ALICE'S ADVENTURES IN
  WONDERLAND (illus)   25p

A complete and unabridged edition of Lewis
Carroll's famous classic, superbly illustrated
with full colour photographs from Josef
Shaftel's major new film, released by 20th
Century Fox and starring Ralph Richardson,
Flora Robson, Spike Milligan and Dudley
Moore.